EBURY P[

FARSIDE

Jaishankar Krishnamurthy is a finance professional with over twenty-five years of experience in India, Dubai and Singapore.

Farside is his first book. He is currently working on three other books: a crime thriller, which he is co-authoring with Dr Anitha Perinchery, set in a psychiatric clinic; a book that takes a deep dive into financial crimes during the 2016 demonetization exercise; and a financial thriller set in Dubai.

He is also the founder of Script A Hit, a unique start-up dedicated to helping the many creative minds like him realize their dreams of becoming authors and audio-visual concept creators.

Jai lives with his wife and their canine children in Bengaluru.

Krishna Udayasankar is the author of The Aryavarta Chronicles (*Govinda*, *Kaurava*, *Kurukshetra* and *The Cowherd Prince*), *3*, *Immortal*, *Objects of Affection* and *Beast*. Her short stories and poems have appeared in multiple anthologies and many of her books have been optioned for screen by leading production houses. She is currently working on two screenplays.

She also leads a social initiative committed to building capacity for dialogue and transformation of conflict across diverse groups in society.

Krishna, who will respond eagerly to 'Khaleesi, Mother of Huskies', lives with her husband and their canine children in Bengaluru.

ALSO BY KRISHNA UDAYASANKAR

FARSIDE

EVERYBODY HAS ANOTHER SIDE

JAISHANKAR
KRISHNAMURTHY

KRISHNA
UDAYASANKAR

EBURY
PRESS

An imprint of Penguin Random House

EBURY PRESS

USA | Canada | UK | Ireland | Australia
New Zealand | India | South Africa | China

Ebury Press is part of the Penguin Random House group of companies
whose addresses can be found at global.penguinrandomhouse.com

Published by Penguin Random House India Pvt. Ltd
4th Floor, Capital Tower 1, MG Road,
Gurugram 122 002, Haryana, India

First published in Ebury Press by Penguin Random House India 2021

ISBN 9780143454175

Typeset in Adobe Caslon Pro by Manipal Technologies Limited, Manipal
Printed at Replika Press Pvt. Ltd, India

www.penguin.co.in

To my wife, who makes dreams come true.

—Jaishankar Krishnamurthy

PART 1

farside (noun): the side of the moon away from the earth
// the lunar farside

—Merriam-Webster Dictionary

1

On any other day, Charu would have wanted to call Ravi, her older brother, a pig for the mess that was his cupboard. She thought for a moment and then whispered the words nevertheless: 'Messy pig.'

It had been two weeks since she had received that midnight call, flown at once to Mumbai, signed for her brother's enshrouded body at a mortuary and cremated it at the break of dawn, all in the span of what felt like a dream. She had not even seen Ravi's face. They had said there was little left to see.

When the lorry had rammed Ravi's car, his head snapped forward and hit the steering wheel. The impact, the report noted, had shattered Ravi's neck. In the hours that followed, the remains of his face had grotesquely swelled up and the cold contents of burst veins bled out from the eyes and nose. Of course, it need not have happened that way. It need not have happened at all, if only Ravi had not been driving completely drunk.

Charu could not understand why the doctor and others would share that piece of information as though they expected it to somehow heal the pain or lessen it. Yes, the accident was Ravi's fault. Yes, he was a stupid fuck for drinking and driving. But that did not change the fact that he was her brother and he was now dead.

It also did not change the fact that there was nothing to do but pick up the pieces and move on. Or at least, try to.

Charu studied herself in the rust-dotted mirror of the cupboard, making a point to notice that her jaw was strong and firm, her shoulders were pulled back in defiance. She was not, she told herself, a weak person. No. She was actually stronger than most, braver and more independent. Ravi had made sure of that. *Oh, hell*. Those were tears in her eyes, after all.

Charu turned away from the mirror, wiping off the errant drop sliding down her cheek before Shakuntala, her mother, could catch sight of it. She paused, making sure that Shakuntala was indeed in the kitchen, seasoning the sambar in her own search for a semblance of normality. Then, Charu got back to packing Ravi's possessions—the more mundane ones—to give to a local charity. Placing a final blue checked shirt in the box, she closed and sealed the carton with brown tape before carrying it out to the living room, where she added it to a neat pile.

'Here.' Shakuntala passed her a cup of tea, her efforts to ignore the growing stack far more heartbreaking than any admission of her loss. Even as Charu feared the awkward moment would lead to yet another breakdown—she was not sure whose—they were, quite literally, saved by the doorbell.

Charu opened the door to find a tall man in a well-cut suit standing outside.

'Hi, I'm Jitesh,' the man introduced himself, though Charu did remember meeting him at her brother's funeral. Jitesh was . . . had been . . . wait—what was the right term to use anyway—Ravi's boss at the television network, where he had worked as a reporter.

Charu invited Jitesh inside. He entered the house, revealing behind him another man, far less elegant and far more stricken by grief. Raju, the office boy at XTV Productions, was someone Charu did not know by name, but would never forget for the way he had sobbed at Ravi's funeral.

'When do you leave?' asked Jitesh as he sat down in the small living room.

Thankful that he did not bother with the inanities of asking how she was—which obviously was far from good—Charu replied, 'Another ten days. The doc says Amma could do with some more rest before a long journey like that, and I still have some of Ravi's affairs—his bank accounts and such—to sort out.'

'David should be able to help you with all that. I finally managed to get through to him through a friend at his channel—QZTV. He was on a story about the human traffic jam on Everest and returned to base camp yesterday. He's on his way back to Mumbai as we speak.'

'David?' Shakuntala bustled out the kitchen, her face showing distinct hope at the sound of the name.

'He'll be here soon, Aunty,' Jitesh informed her, even as Charu maintained an expressionless impatience.

David. Ravi's best friend. The best friend whom she had never met. The one her mother had been asking for every day for two weeks now. Somehow, much as she was sure David was a nice person, Charu had decided that she did not want to like him; all the more so now for the relief on Shakuntala's face as she returned to the kitchen with renewed energy, saying she would make tea for the visitors.

A silence followed Shakuntala's departure, punctuated only by the muted sounds of a neighbour's TV. Jitesh sighed, then took an envelope from the inside pocket of his jacket and handed it over to Charu.

He said, 'It's not much. The post-mortem report and the police report have declared it a case of drunken driving. The insurance company says it can't pay out in this case. This . . . this is from XTV productions. As much as I could get the management to agree on as compensation. I'm sorry . . . I know Ravi could not have left much savings behind, with your mother's treatments and all. I just hope . . .'

'We'll be fine,' Charu declared, though she did not turn down the package. 'I graduate in less than a year and I already have a job lined up for after, from my last internship. We just need to manage for a bit and then it will all be fine.'

'He always said you were a tough girl. He was very proud of you, you know?'

Charu started at the unexpected compliment. She looked up at Jitesh, taking in the dash of grey at his temples that gave him a refined—and undoubtedly attractive—look. She chuckled silently, amused that she could notice such a thing at such a moment.

'Thank you, Jitesh.'

'And if there's anything you need, anything at all, Charu . . .' Jitesh scrawled his personal phone number and his address on the back of his business card and handed it to her.

'Thank you,' Charu repeated.

Looking up just to break away from Jitesh's intense but far from discomfiting gaze, Charu turned to Raju. 'Arre. Why are you standing? Please sit,' she said.

Raju mumbled excuses of preferring to stand, but Charu realized it was a matter of hierarchy: the office boy could not, would not, sit on the same sofa as his boss.

Charu got up and pulled out a chair from the set around the dining table. 'Please sit, Raju *bhaiyya*.'

At a nod of permission from Jitesh, Raju took the proffered seat, crumpling into it in tears. 'Madam, you are just like your brother. So kind. So friendly. Always wanting to help. Even that day . . . that day . . . I asked Ravi sir where he was going and he said he was leaving early because he was going to donate blood at the hospital. But he reached there as a dead body. *Hey Bhagwan*! How can you do this to a good person . . .'

Charu felt a pang of unease, a niggling doubt, but before she could figure out what it was, Raju began bawling.

She cast a look towards the kitchen, then a more plaintive glance at Jitesh, who immediately understood. Standing up, he began to usher the mourning Raju out of the house and into the corridor.

'Call me if you need anything,' he told Charu as he bundled Raju into the lift.

Closing the front door, Charu made her way into the kitchen. 'They left,' she told Shakuntala, helping herself to one of the cups of tea that her mother had made. 'Jitesh got an urgent call.'

Shakuntala frowned at Charu's excessive consumption of tea but the gesture was met with a mischievous wink. She sighed and picked up the other cup for herself. 'When did he say David was getting here?'

The question prompted a sneer from Charu. *David*. The sneer became a sigh as Charu admitted to herself that despite the WhatsApp forwards and weekly phone calls, she had lost track of Ravi's life over the past four years, of how he had managed work, their ailing mother, his own love life. Hell, did he even have one? She could not say. She knew near nothing about his friends, especially his best buddy David.

It was, she supposed, typical of her brother, that he rarely talked about himself. He had always been the over-protective type, the paternal figure she had needed when their father had died. He had made sure that it was always about her and her happiness.

Ravi had barely been nineteen or so and she on the brink of her teens, when Appa had passed on. Ravi had dropped out of the Indian Institute of Technology (IIT) Kanpur without a second thought and begun working to support them, making sure that Charu got everything he did not, including the engineering degree that he had had to give up. Through it all, Ravi had remained a cheerful, unresentful man, flitting from one job to another to make ends meet till finally, XTV Productions had realized that degree or not, Ravi was a whiz with visuals. They had offered him a job, which he had taken, only to then accidentally discover his love for reporting.

His career had taken wing after that, as had his entire life. He had made friends, bought the bike that he wanted— not the one he could just about afford—and acquired the latest PlayStation and a large LED TV to go with it. He had even placed a down payment on the small but elegant flat he and Shakuntala had moved into, the rest being cleared in monthly instalments that he could finally afford.

At last, Ravi had started making up for the years he had lost in his forced role as a father to his sister.

At that admission, Charu realized that it was not David she was pissed with. It was herself, for having cocooned herself away comfortably in a foreign land, leaving Ravi to his struggles—mundane or otherwise. She was two years short of thirty, already a smart, reputed visual effects designer and yet, she had been happy to play the role of a kid sister and spoilt daughter.

'Eh, Charu, I asked you when David gets here,' Shakuntala repeated.

'Jitesh said today or tomorrow, Amma.'

'He'll come here straight from the station or airport or wherever it is; you'll see. He'll come straight to see me. If only he'd been around that day, he'd have taken care of Ravi. Our Ravi would still be with us . . .'

Her quota of stoicism done for the day, Shakuntala broke into tears. Charu hesitated, unsure of what she ought to do. Then she wrapped her arms around Shakuntala, letting the older woman bury her face against her stomach and cry without restraint as Charu whispered meaningless consolations that she herself longed to hear.

It felt strange sleeping in her brother's bed. Not that Charu had not done it before. Right from the days she had been working in Bangalore, whenever she visited what had then been a musty old rental apartment, Ravi would insist on giving her his room and plonking himself on the sofa, just to have the delight of being inordinately loud in the morning as he got ready for work and then teasing her about what a lazy bum she was being when she complained about it. But this was the first time she was in *this* house—the flat that he had bought and owned—and to sleep there knowing that he was gone, that this was no affectionate sibling rivalry but an irreversible fact of life, was different. It was also a long-winded way of explaining to herself why she could not sleep.

Charu had stayed up as late as she could justify, clearing out Ravi's desk, disposing of his papers, electricity and gas bills, gym membership cards, movie theatre loyalty vouchers and the many administrative minutiae of life. The police had returned his wallet, surprisingly with cash, credit cards and ID cards still inside, though they claimed they had not been able to find his phone and laptop. Charu supposed it had been 'lost' in the evidence room and some stranger was now the owner of a near-new smartphone and a high-end laptop. Still, it was a small loss considering . . .

She waited till her mother had fallen into a drug-induced sleep to take down two whole bags of a life well-lived, soon to be reduced to garbage. Then she came back upstairs and curled up in Ravi's bed. But as her phone gleamed an indisputable 3 a.m. and sleep showed no signs of favouring her, she threw herself out of bed and made her way to the cupboard where she knew her brother kept his favourite single malt. She pulled out the bottle and poured herself a drink. The sip became a shot as she threw it down her throat in one go and poured herself another glass.

And that was when it struck.

Charu had just about enough presence of mind to pick up the keys to the front door off the dining table, but she bothered neither with slippers nor a change of attire as she ran out of the house in her pyjamas and pressed the lift button. Inside, she pounded the button for the basement car park—which also housed the garbage recycling area.

The basement was effectively deserted, the single watchman on duty snoring in his chair by the entrance.

Charu ignored him and made her way into the depths of the parking lot, to the corner where numerous plastic bags awaited collection by the city's sanitation workers in the morning. Steeling herself against the odour, she began opening the bags one by one with an urgency, ignoring even the urge to curse the residents who did not believe in garbage segregation.

'Yikes!' Charu shrieked as a scavenging cockroach crawled up her arm. She swatted the offending creature off and—deciding against stomping it—continued to look through the bags of piled up refuse. At last, Charu found what she was looking for: the garbage bag filled with stuff from Ravi's desk that she had decided to throw away.

Carrying the bag to a corner of the parking lot where a tube light shone intermittently, Charu emptied its contents on the floor and began sifting through them.

'Yes!' Charu cried out as she found what it was that she was looking for. Hands trembling, she pieced together the plastic card she had cut into two barely hours ago and stared at it, recalling what Raju had said earlier that day that bothered her . . . and at what it might imply. 'You wouldn't, Ravi,' she said to herself in the eclectic dimness. 'You would never . . .' She picked up the pieces, clutching them close even as she tried to come to terms with all that it meant.

She did not notice the figure watching her from the shadows till it slowly moved forward to stand right beside her. As a heavy hand descended on her shoulder, Charu screamed.

2

Naina Mathur looked fresh and energetic despite the early hour. She also appeared completely unperturbed by the swollen cadaver that lay on the banks of the creek from which it had been recovered barely an hour ago. Whatever clothes the deceased may have once worn had since torn off to reveal putrefying blue and grey nakedness, now masked partially by a plastic sheet. Naina lifted up the sheet—clearly a nearby find and not a police issue—with a loud complaint about contaminated crime scenes and a pointed look at the three constables in attendance.

The men carried expressions of disgust and revulsion in their eyes and handkerchiefs over their noses and mouths, though the cloth did little against the omnipresent odour. Giving them a look of disapproval as she pulled on her gloves, Naina settled down to work.

'He's been in the water for at least two weeks,' she said out loud, moving aside a flap of disintegrating skin to get a clearer look at the bones underneath.

'Suicide case,' the senior constable declared.

Naina smirked to herself at his smug tone. She may well have outranked him—junior forensic analyst that she was—but was well-used to condescension and dismissal. *Not this time*, she decided, making a mental note to cement the reputation the incident could possibly get her.

She threw back the sheet covering the cadaver to display its decomposition in all its gory glory.

Immediately, sounds of choking and gagging escaped from the throats of the junior cops on the scene. One of them left to throw up. The other man went with him to help, leaving the senior constable no choice but to stay and face his embarrassment.

'*Yeh* suicide *nahin hai*, madam,' a voice piped up. 'This is not a suicide.'

Naina turned to see a local man, dressed in a banian that had seen whiter days and a faded lungi, hovering nearby.

The constable interjected, 'Arre! Not a suicide? You know better than madam, *kya*? Let madam decide.' He then said to Naina, by way of explanation. 'This man found the body. He lives in that slum nearby and came out to . . . to answer nature's call. The *big* call. Or so he claims. That's when he found the body.'

'Uh huh,' Naina responded, uninterested in the man's bowel movements.

'Nahin sir,' the man persisted. 'Suicide bodies wash up farther north along the coast. Not in this backwater stream. They jump off the rocks at Lovers' Point and the current . . .'

'Shut up, you fool!'

'He's right,' Naina cut in. 'The victim's bones are broken. Drowning doesn't do that. This guy was beaten up before he was pushed into the water. Whether he was dead or alive when he went in, I'll know after a full post-mortem.' She pulled out her phone and typed into it before adding, 'Based on tide patterns and the fact that he has been in the water this long, it looks like this man fell or was thrown in about two-to-three kilometres south of this backwater creek.'

The local responded with a satisfied grin, even as the constable tried to reassert his authority by asking him, 'What's in that area? Do you know? Or you've never taken a crap there?'

'Sir, they don't allow us there. That area is full of private bungalows. Security is very tight. They don't like us hanging around. Even in the resorts, where the beach is supposed to be public, they keep chasing us off. Of course, they cannot chase out important men like you . . .'

If the cop caught the sarcasm, he also knew well there was nothing he could do about it, at least not at the moment.

He watched sullenly, now rejoined by his fellow policeman, as Naina took measurements, signalling to the photographer waiting in the wings to come forward and also do his job.

'Take down his name and address,' she told the senior constable, gesturing to the local. She added, 'Is the inspector coming? Do we need to wait for him?'

'No, madam. It's too early in the morning for him.'

Naina rolled her eyes. 'All right then, you can load the body into the van. I'm done here. I'll finish the rest of the examination at the mortuary.'

The driver of the van stepped forward to pick up the body, inviting assistance from the policemen with a glance. The two junior constables made a hasty exit in search of yet another tree to vomit behind.

With a sigh and a grumble about how his day would go given that it began with touching a rotting corpse, the senior constable helped the driver load the body into the van, trying not to flinch as seawater and offal stained his uniform in the process.

'All talk, till they see a body. You'd think they're kids, not cops,' Naina muttered to herself. With a last look at the scene and a nod at the still-hovering local, she piled into the passenger seat of the van. She shut her eyes in the hope of catching up on sleep on the long drive back.

3

Charu was vaguely aware, thanks to her neighbour's loud TV habits, that a dead body had washed up somewhere during the night and a police investigation was on, but she paid no attention to it, focused as she was on the man before her.

David.

Hardly had Shakuntala seen David than she had thrown herself into his arms, sobbing vigorously, pouring out every bit of the grief in her heart. For the next two hours, Charu had not known what to do except make endless cups of tea, most of which had gone ignored.

Sipping loudly on her most recent—and still hot—cup of tea, Charu took a good look at the much-fêted, much-lauded David. He was a strikingly handsome man; she gave him that. But he was also such a stark contrast to Ravi that she simply could not understand why her mother treated him as a second son.

Where Ravi had been elegant and understated, David seemed to be the kind of man who lived in the heavy-metal T-shirt and jeans he was now wearing. He was tall, as Ravi had been, but square-jawed and rugged, compared to Ravi's statuesque, clean-shaved charm. David's hair had an I-don't-care wavy length to it, whereas Ravi had always been fastidious about his haircuts, and where Ravi would probably have consoled the sobbing Shakuntala with words of reason and philosophy, David was whispering tender assurances, holding Shakuntala close and patting her cheek.

Was David perhaps the more attentive, expressive son that Ravi had not been? But that was not fair, Charu told herself. Ravi had done everything and more for them; if he had not had time or energy to be a doting mama's boy, that was because he had been busy working hard to provide for them. Surely Shakuntala knew that? Or perhaps she had until this *charmer* had waltzed in and . . .

Charu cut short her irritated evaluations as David helped Shakuntala to her feet. Shakuntala did not as much as glance at Charu as she allowed David to escort her to her room to rest.

Charu scowled at her now-empty cup, trying to prioritize the events of the night and what needed to be done next over the feeling of being a stranger to her own family. She was only partly successful. She was still scowling when, a little later, David sat down opposite her at the dining table.

'You don't like me.'

Charu had prepared herself for many possible openings to the inevitable conversation, but this she had not foreseen.

'No,' she admitted, feeling far too worn out for politeness.

David grinned. 'Is that why you screamed when you saw me earlier, in the basement?'

'I screamed because you startled me, lurking up on me in the darkness like that. You're just lucky I didn't hit you with something. And if you think you're being funny harping on that, I assure you it's not going to make me like you any better.'

'You're right; it's not funny.' David let what had clearly been a fake smile fade from his lips. He reached out for the pieces of plastic that Charu had recovered the previous night, now reassembled into a whole to reveal a blood donor's card with Ravi's name and photograph on it. 'You're right.'

'You just said that.'

'I mean about the accident, Charu,' David said, tapping a long finger on the donor card. 'If Ravi had been going to donate blood, there's no way he would have had even a drop of alcohol in him. But when I spoke to him on the phone that evening . . . at around six o'clock or so . . . he mentioned nothing about drinking nor the blood donation. Still . . .'

A heavy silence fell over them both, marred by the music indicating the ending of the morning news on the neighbour's TV.

Taking a deep breath, Charu asked, 'Can you help me, David? Can you help me figure out what really happened? Will you come with me to the police station?'

'You don't have to ask, Charu. Just because I'm not crying my eyes out doesn't mean I don't . . . did not . . . love Ravi. Whether you intend to or not, I certainly mean to get to the bottom of this whole thing . . . and you don't have to like me for it,' he added, flipping the pieces of the card back on to the table.

'Is that reverse psychology?'

'It's whatever-the-fuck-you-want-it-to-be. Now, I'm making myself some proper south Indian filter coffee, not your crappy American chai latte tea. Want some?'

The police station offered little atmosphere for conversation, not that Charu was in a mood to make any. David seemed to be of like mind, asking once if he could get her something to drink, maybe a bottle of mineral water? Other than that, he maintained a stolid silence, moving now and then to send an occasional message or email from his phone, but for the most part staying absolutely still, watching everything that was going on in the police station.

The inspector in charge of the case, they had been informed, was out attending to another matter. Charu had tried to ask when he might be back, but David had taken the information in stride, settling down to wait on a narrow wooden bench set against a wall. Sighing, Charu had sat down next to him, crossing her arms in an attempt to not fidget. At first, she looked expectantly at every uniformed figure who entered the station, then gave up, settling into annoyed inactivity.

After two hours of waiting, Charu was about to get up from her seat, compelled by a mix of impatience and a growing need to find a bathroom—clean or otherwise—when she noticed a constable pointing her out to a figure she had not noticed entering the premises. She and David stood as the inspector made his way towards them.

'Sorry you had to wait,' the man said, though he looked anything but contrite as he gestured towards the chairs in front of his table. Settling himself into his own, more-comfortable chair, the inspector adjusted the thick towel placed against the Rexine, then proceeded to pray to a small Ganesha statue placed on his desk, before eventually returning his attention to the waiting Charu and David.

'How can I help you, madam?'

'Sir, I wanted to enquire about my brother's . . . his case.'

'Your brother's case?' The inspector shook his head at her obvious naiveté in assuming that of the many brothers and many cases on his desk, he would know which one was hers. 'Tell me the name, madam.'

'Ravi Srinivasan.'

'Your name, madam?'

'Charulata Srinivasan.'

'South Indian?'

The inspector stated the obvious, to which Charu nodded. The officer then turned his attention to David. 'Who are you?'

'David Fernandes. I'm a friend.'

As the inspector gave David a look of disdainful appraisal, Charu once again found herself missing Ravi and his officious, gentlemanly presence.

But David apparently passed muster, for the inspector called out to a constable. 'Bring me that drunk-death case file, that highway-*waala* accident.'

Charu kept her eyes on her fingers as she dug them into the fabric of her tote bag, trying not to grimace at the policeman's tone. Out of the corner of her eye, she saw David lift his hand off his knee, as though he meant to place it on her arm. Instead, he shifted, and let it come down on the back of his chair.

Meanwhile, the inspector shuffled through the file that had been brought to him before declaring: 'Ah yes. Simple case, madam. Sorry for your loss, by the way. The post-mortem report showed high alcohol content in your brother's blood. We have closed the case.'

'Closed it?' Charu was aghast. 'But . . . what about the lorry driver? Did you question him? Was *he* tested for drunk driving? How can we be so sure it was Ravi's fault? My brother was a very careful person, Inspector. He wasn't irresponsible like that, he would never . . .'

The inspector held up a hand, following it up with a condescending look as Charu fell silent. 'Madam, I understand your pain. Losing the only man in the house . . . the head of a household . . . tch . . . very, very difficult . . . especially for the ladies. But *kya karein* . . . the evidence is clear. As for questioning the lorry driver, no need, madam. Anyway, the fellow ran away from the accident site. Not because it was his fault, mind you, but because he was a thief. The lorry owner reported the vehicle as stolen the next morning as soon as it was not found in its usual parking spot. So you tell me, how to question the driver fellow? We don't even know who he is.'

Charu persisted. 'All right. What about the lorry owner? You have his details, right? Did you question him? Was the vehicle in proper condition? Can I see the inspection certificate?'

'Not allowed, madam.'

'But—'

'What to do, madam. Rules are rules,' he finished, with a smile that dripped fake sympathy.

'But I have a right to—' Charu stopped short as this time, David did lay a light hand on her arm. He then leaned forward and handed over a press identification card to the inspector.

The inspector waved it away, 'Arre, it makes no difference.'

'Please take a look, inspector. Please,' David said.

The inspector frowned and reached forward to take the ID card, his face lighting up with recognition as he felt the texture of a crisp currency note folded under the card. He brought the card closer to his chest in a show of inspecting it and then returned the ID to David after smoothly pocketing the money with his free hand.

'Thank you for understanding,' the inspector declared, standing up. 'Now, I am very busy and have other matters to attend to. Namaste.' He made a show of closing the file and placing it on the table before walking away.

Charu did not waste any time on shock and pulled the file towards her. David felt around in his pockets for a pen, but Charu pulled out her phone and began snapping photos of every page and paper in the file. She forced herself not to look at the photos of the accident scene, letting her mind blur over the images of Ravi's mangled body in the driver's seat as she kept going, making sure she got every detail in the file. With that done, she closed the file and placed it neatly in the middle of the table.

The two left the police station, David pausing to shake the inspector's hand and passing him yet another two-thousand-rupee note in thanks.

Charu did not speak till she and David were back in his jeep, modest for its obvious second-hand status, but still quite a stylish ride. Then she began in a rush: 'This is crap. There is no way Ravi was drunk and got into an accident. This is a cover-up. Sheer incompetence. And I won't let it go unquestioned. We can get the CBI involved. We'll file a lawsuit. And we can reach out to the media. Wait, you're a media person. You can do that, can't you? Get this whole mess on the news? David? David, are you even listening to me?'

She went from excited to frustrated as she took in David's posture, his expression. He had not started the vehicle but sat with his hands on the wheel, gazing into the distance, seeming completely uninterested in her words. Gritting her teeth against rising anger, she spat out, 'Do you even care, David?'

The words triggered a reaction, but hardly one that Charu expected.

Without looking at her, David pulled out his phone and dialed a number. 'Hello, could I please speak to Anand Uncle? David here. Oh hi, Manju Didi, hope you are well. And the kids? Yes, I'm fine. I actually . . . okay.'

Silence, as David waited for someone to come on the phone. Then he said, 'Hi Uncle, David here. A friend of mine needs your help. Her brother, my friend Ravi . . . don't know if I've mentioned him . . . I have, is it? Okay. Ravi died recently in an accident, but the whole thing is very suspicious. We have the case details. Could you please help us?'

He listened as the person on the other end spoke, ostensibly giving instructions on the next steps, then signed off with, 'Okay, we'll see you there at 4 p.m., then. Thanks, Uncle. And Uncle, the advance will be . . . no, no, Uncle. A job is a job. Just glad that this one is in your hands.'

David hung up, started the jeep and began driving without looking at Charu or meeting her questioning gaze. She glared at him for a few moments before giving up and turning away towards the window. She closed her eyes against the bright sunlight, but the moment she did, images of Ravi as she imagined he might have been in his last moments—bloody, dying painfully, waiting for help that never came—flashed against the black.

Charu's eyes flew open and remained that way as she squinted at the sun, wishing the harsh glare could erase what she had just seen with her mind's eye.

4

Charu walked into the designated coffee shop—the name and location of which had been the only words David had spoken to her as he had dropped her home—to find him already there and in conversation with a silver-haired gentleman she placed at about sixty-five years. Despite her immediate self-caution against first impressions, Charu was disappointed. His nondescript frame and kind eyes were his own, but the half-sleeved shirt, pants and slippers combination was almost expected of his generation. Indeed, he looked more like someone's genial uncle than he did anyone who could help them. Still, Charu greeted him with a namaste and took a seat at the table.

David made the introductions: 'Charu, Anand Uncle . . . Anand sir is a retired policeman. His investigative record is spectacular. He now deals with select cases as a private detective. He is an old friend of my father's, so he offered to help us for free. But—'

Charu immediately dismissed the notion with thanks. 'I will be more than happy to honour your professional fees, sir. I just hope that you can help me.'

'I've already told Anand Uncle what happened, briefed him on the post-mortem report and the blood donor card; everything right up to this morning's visit to the police station,' David said.

'And?' Charu sat forward. 'What do you think, sir?'

Anand glanced at David, then leaned forward, mirroring Charu's stance. 'The question here is not what happened, Ms Charu, but what we can do about it.'

'What do you mean? And please, call me Charu.'

'Okay, Charu. Based on everything David has just told me, I think it's more than possible that the accident was not a case of drunk driving. It may very well have been reckless driving on the lorry driver's part, and the lorry owner has tampered with the investigation to ensure that his transport licence is not affected.'

'Tampered? How?'

'Anything from bribing the doctor conducting the post-mortem report to changing the blood samples. I've even seen alcohol being injected into bodies . . . post-mortem.' He gave David yet another glance, this one apologetic.

Charu did not appear to catch on to Anand's pessimism. 'So we can find out how they did it. We can prove that Ravi did not cause the accident, that it was actually the lorry driver's fault.' She dived into her purse and came up with an envelope. 'Please start at once, sir. And spare no expense. I want these fuckers—sorry—these criminals brought to justice.'

Anand did not seem to care in the least about her use of the expletive or the envelope before him. He said, 'And then what? Let's say we can somehow show that the report was tampered with. Half the drivers employed these days don't have proper papers. Let's say we can even find the lorry driver in question—though I'm guessing he has returned to his village by now—and get him to admit no fault on your brother's part. What are we going to get out of it?'

'If we can show Ravi was not drunk, he was not at fault, we can sue the transport company for wrongful death.'

'And? Do you know how long that will take? Or how many rounds of the courts you will have to make before you see a verdict? David tells me you and your mother are planning to leave for the US soon; that you're doing your post-graduation degree there. Are you going to leave your life in the US and come sit in India to see this case through? And what are you expecting to get out of a verdict, even if it goes in your favour? I don't think you care about compensation or money. Are you going to throw your whole life away—and probably put your mother through hell too—just to prove that Ravi was not an irresponsible drunk driver?'

Anand gently pushed the envelope back towards her. 'I understand your pain, Charu. More than the pain, I understand the anger. But as someone who has spent more than forty years on the job, I'm telling you, this is . . . well, I won't say it's not worth it, because what you've lost is beyond value. But I will say that it is futile.'

Charu sat back, grasping for words at her helplessness, at what Anand had clearly described as the impracticality of her ideas. Grudgingly, she admitted that he was right; it would not be a rational thing to do—to give up on a whim the life that Ravi had made sure she could have. It would not be fair to her mother. It was not what Ravi would have wanted.

Ravi.

Charu shut her eyes against the tears that threatened as yet more images of Ravi flashed through her mind. Ravi laughing, Ravi proud and jubilant the day she got her admission to the Massachusetts Institute of Technology (MIT), Ravi tucking her into bed as though she were a child, telling her to go for it, make her dreams—and his— come true. Ravi, waving to her before he had walked into Boston airport two years ago. She had never seen his face in person again, not even in death. Her last sight of Ravi had been that of a cadaver wrapped up from head to toe in a white sheet. Charu felt her heart implode. She thought she was about to scream out loud right there when she felt a strong hand over hers.

Was it Ravi's hand; please, could that be his hand? Could it be that this was all just a bad dream and that she would wake up to find her quiet, loving brother looking at her, ready to tease her for what was nothing more than her morbid imagination?

No, this hand was warmer, heavier, but somehow just as reassuring. Charu opened her eyes to find a resolute David looking at her. She blinked away the tears and was about to say she was all right and she did not need his sympathy, when he turned away to address Anand.

'We can decide what to do with the evidence and findings, such as they are, later. For now, Uncle, I think it's important we find out exactly what happened. Futile or not, I think we need to know. I think Charu deserves to know.'

Anand looked from David to Charu, taking in the determination and surprise on their respective faces. 'All right,' he said. 'Charu, I believe you took photos of the case file at the police station. Could you please WhatsApp me those pictures? This is my number.' Anand showed her the screen of his phone.

'Oh yes, at once, sir,' Charu said, then paused as she realized David's hand still lay over hers. He seemed to have realized this too, for he quickly moved it away and turned his attention to his barely touched coffee.

'All right then,' Anand said, standing up to leave. Charu and David followed suit out of politeness, but Anand waved at them to remain seated. 'I'll call you at the earliest.'

'Thank you, sir,' Charu said. She pushed the envelope towards Anand. 'I hope this covers at least the expenses. I'm happy to transfer . . .' She left the offer hanging as Anand looked at her with a paternal smile. Then he shook his head, pocketed the envelope and left the café.

Charu threw herself back in her seat and gasped loudly, as though she had been holding her breath in all the while. Then she looked at David. 'Thank you.'

'Don't be silly . . . . come on, I'll drop you home.'

'I can take a cab.'

David looked as though she had cracked a bad joke. 'Don't be silly.'

'Is that your stock line?'

'Nope,' David said, as Charu paid the bill and they stood up to leave. 'My stock line is: Don't be *fucking* silly.'

5

The men looked like they could have been any two of the many delivery boys, electricians, loaders or general workers who went in and out of the mall housing the café that Charu and David had just exited. But there was a clear intent and caution about their every move that suggested these two were more than everyday tradesmen going about their work though, in a sense, that was exactly what they were.

They fell in behind Charu and David, initially following them from a distance of over thirty feet, without once losing sight of their quarry or moving in any manner that could seem suspicious to an onlooker. Indeed, most of the mall goers ignored them, as did David and Charu. When Charu pressed the lift button to head to the basement parking lot where David had left his car, the men got in too. 'Side please,' one of them said.

When the lift reached the basement, the two men were the first to exit, walking purposefully away before anyone else could move. Moving silently, seamlessly, the two doubled back from different directions, weaving through the cars to a spot they had carefully chosen earlier, not ten feet away from where David was parked. Their targets, however, still stood near the lift, engaged in indistinct but animated conversation.

One of the men, a thin, youngish fellow, who presumably was the junior on the job, looked to the other. His companion shook his head, indicating with a glance to a cobweb-laced security camera on one of the pillars. They would have to wait till David and Charu came to the blind spot that had been selected to make their move.

David and Charu resumed walking, still intent on their conversation. Snatches of it came floating through to the two men. '. . . Anand Uncle *will* get the job done, Charu. I thought you were okay with this . . .'

'If you say so, David. Frankly, I was a little disappointed by his attitude. But I can't think of what else to do, so I suppose he is what we have for now.'

They were closer now, and the waiting men could hear them distinctly. The one in charge remained ready but calm, while the other one crouched, like an animal waiting to pounce.

David was saying, 'Like it or not, Charu, he has a point. But you're right, even I want to give this a shot, the best shot we can . . .' He pulled out his remote-controlled car key and pressed a button, unlocking his vehicle with a beep.

The men moved.

The booming sound of fast-beat music mingled with a loud screech filled the air as an imported SUV zoomed down the entry ramp at excessive speed, then stepped on the brakes as the driver hit the curve leading into the parking lot. David and Charu looked up, then jumped aside between the parked vehicles, as the SUV zoomed past them into the depths of the basement.

'Motherfucker!' David and Charu cursed in union at the presumably yuppie driver, then exchanged tentative smiles. David led Charu out from behind the row of parked cars towards his jeep.

The thugs hesitated; their quarry had cut around the blind spot to remerge in a zone covered by cameras. Besides, the whole parking lot now seemed more alert and vibrant, with several shoppers in the parking lot being shocked out of their self-absorbed solitude by the errant SUV. The subordinate thug took a step forward, mistaking his senior's forbearance for reluctance. He was made to back down by a frown.

The men waited as they were and watched David pull out of the parking lot on his way towards the exit. 'They got away,' the subordinate said, quite unnecessarily.

'Never mind. We know where to find them. And when we do . . .' His accomplice smiled. It was not pleasant.

6

The Retired Police Officer's Colony was a small haven
in the middle of a bustling suburb. Blocks of low-rise
apartments clustered together, fringed by a city rarity of
green trees and flowering shrubs, while grey high-rises
towered on the edges of the colony, looking down at the
unassailable pocket of high-value real estate.

Anand cleared away the remains of breakfast, enjoying
the fulfilled silence his family had left in its wake after
departing for their respective schools and workplaces. He
made himself another cup of tea before settling down at
the computer in a corner of the small living room. He
allowed himself one more smile of self-satisfaction as he
navigated his way on the Internet to Facebook and then his
email account. He dutifully read through all the spam mails
in his inbox (personal loan in five minutes, no documents
required; a lovely widow from Nigeria who needed help
with the billions she had inherited from her recently
deceased husband; pills for weight loss and weight gain),
before deleting them, but not without making a note that
now that he was able to type with the index fingers of both

hands. Perhaps it was time to indulge in an iPad, bought on interest-free instalments, of course. He had just logged out of the computer and switched off the system when he heard a cheery voice at the still-open door.

'Hi, Uncle!'

'Naina!' Anand received the young policewoman with a wide smile. 'Come in, come in.'

Naina slipped off her sandals at the door and came in, holding a steel container. 'Aai made ladoos,' she said, gesturing generally in the direction of the block of flats located directly opposite. 'Sent some for you.'

Anand eagerly accepted the container, invitingly warm from the just-made contents. He overcame the desire to sample the sweets at once and—setting the container down on the coffee table—urged Naina to one of the sofas.

'Night duty?' he asked as they both sat down.

Naina replied with a roll of her eyes and an exaggerated sigh, 'Yes, and I need to head back in soon.'

'How is work going?'

'Hectic, Uncle. A body washed up in one of the backwater creeks two nights ago. It's a mess! Sometimes I wonder what on earth made me go into forensics.'

'You're your father's daughter. Deshpande was one of the best investigators we had. Of course, back then, we didn't have much of forensics to help us out. It was good old-fashioned footwork and deduction.'

'Which is what made me fall in love with it, remember?'

'Oh yes,' Anand said, smiling fondly at the memories of a five-year-old Naina borrowing his uniform cap to play pretend policewoman. 'You know, your mother has never forgiven us—your father and me—for letting you hang around when we discussed our cases. But you used to be so eager to solve them, as though they were puzzles.' He laughed and added, 'Still game for that?'

Naina laughed in turn and said, 'Always! What do you have for me, Uncle?'

Anand pulled out his phone and showed her a series of photos. He waited as Naina studied the photos and then asked her, 'All right, madam investigator. Accident or murder?'

Naina gave him a look of mock scorn. 'You already know what it is, don't you? You're just messing with me?'

'Am I?'

'All right then, Uncle. See here. These dents on the side of the car? The way the metal is crushed shows that the impact was from one direction alone. This car was not moving when the other vehicle—a bus or lorry, basically something big—rammed it.'

'So the accident was staged?'

'Yes. As far as I can tell. I could be sure if I got to see the vehicle for myself, but I am pretty confident about this part of it.'

'So, murder,' Anand grimly concluded. 'Someone rammed this car on purpose.'

'Well, it is murder, but not for that reason. I mean, theoretically, it is possible that a driver lost control of his vehicle and rammed a parked car. But wait, look at this . . .' She swiped forward on Anand's phone to another photograph. 'The driver's seat has a bloodstain pattern that suggests a big injury to the back of the head. Unlikely in the case of an accident like this one, where the car was rammed on the side; the occupant's neck would snap and fall forward or to the side. Also, the size of the bloodstain suggests your victim was in that seat for a long time after he started bleeding. Do you know how long it took for the first responders to get to the scene? That could confirm things. Of course,' Naina said, placing the phone down on the coffee table, 'this is the best I can do without seeing the car or the body. What did the post-mortem show?'

'They found high levels of alcohol in the victim's blood, so it was treated as a drunk-driving case,' Anand replied.

'Well, it's always possible that the victim got drunk, got into a fight, made it back to his car and passed out and then was accidentally hit by another vehicle. That would rule out wilful murder but then it would mean that the victim had really, really bad luck. Too many assumptions needed there.'

'Occam's Razor. Your father swore by it.'

'Yeah, he managed to memorize the Latin version of it and used it to piss off your senior officers. I remember you telling me that. More than once, in fact. On that note, I'd better get going, Uncle.'

'Give your parents my regards. And a special thanks to your mom for the sweets. Manju has put me on a strict diet, but I'll definitely find a way to enjoy them!'

Naina wagged her finger in mock caution before picking up her bag and leaving.

Anand briefly studied the box of sweets in a half-hearted attempt at forbearance before finally opening the lid and popping an entire ladoo into his mouth. He sat back, savouring the delicacy to its last crumb, and then made to reach for another, but restrained himself. With a sigh, he closed the lid on the box and picked up his phone. He swiped through the photos he had shown Naina. Her expertise had confirmed some of his suspicions regarding Ravi's death, but had also given rise to many new questions.

Flipping open the box again, Anand popped yet another forbidden ladoo into his mouth. The taste stayed on his tongue long after he had locked up and left the house.

Anand's destination was a good forty-five minutes away by local train, and he spent the time dozing lightly, lulled into thoughtless bliss by the clatter of wheels on rails. Allowing himself a break for some strong tea from a roadside stall, he arrived at one of the booking offices of Mehra Transports—the company that owned the lorry involved in Ravi's accident—fresh and ready for the gentle farce that lay ahead.

Through the glass front of the office, such as it was, Anand could see the seated 'manager' engaged in the middle of fervently dressing down a hapless-looking employee. This, Anand realized, was going to be easier than he had expected.

'Eh! Useless fellow! Putting diesel inside yourself as well, is it. *Aai shapat*, one day I will . . .' The man seated

behind the old Sunmica-covered table cut short his tirade
as Anand entered the tiny booking office. The lungi-clad
lorry driver, who had clearly been the subject of the other
man's ire, took the chance to make a hasty exit. The booking
manager scowled at the departing man, then rearranged his
features into a smile as he greeted Anand. 'Sir, please come,
take your seat. Sorry about that. But you know how these
fellows can be so . . . unreliable.'

'Unreliable?' Anand took on an expression of mild
panic, playing his intended role to perfection.

'No, no, sir. Not all of them. Sometimes. These
Madrasi fellows . . . Sir, you are from which state, sir?' he
enquired, realizing that he might be adding to the damage
instead of ameliorating it.

'Why? I look like an outsider, is it?' Despite the words,
Anand sat back in his chair in a show of reassured solidarity
that made the office manager heave a sigh of relief.

The manager, deciding against the risk of more small
talk, got straight to the point. 'Yes sir, how may I be of
service?'

'I need to hire a water tanker. Daily. For my housing
society. I am the society president, you see. But I need a
reliable fellow. If there's no water in the buildings, the
residents will heap abuses on me. Then who will answer?
Your fellows are reliable? You are sure, no?'

'Sir, I assure you . . .'

Over the next half hour—through a series of innocuous
questions that appeared to do little more than reassure the
self-declared president of a non-existent Bharat Housing

Society of the reliability of the water delivery services he was intent on engaging and admissions of regional xenophobia that he did not at all feel—Anand was able to extract all the information he required.

At length, he got up from his chair, saying, 'I will speak to my other committee members and get back to you in a day or two.'

'Most definitely, sir. And please do come back to us. I will give you the best rates. In fact, if you can come back before evening, I can speak to my boss and get him to extend a 5 per cent discount. He is leaving the city on business tomorrow morning, so . . .'

Anand feigned residual chariness. 'You mean you can lower the charges even more? But you said you were giving me the best rate? Maybe I should speak to your boss . . . Our society's water requirements are quite high, as I told you.'

The booking manager quickly admitted defeat. 'No, no, sir. Any time you come, I will give you the best rates. That's why I mentioned the discount. Sir, trust me, sir . . .'

'Okay, okay. I will come back after discussing.'

Anand stepped out of the booking office, a smile playing at the corners of his lips at the thought of the self-cursing, consternated manager he had left behind. Playing the cantankerous, over-cautious retiree had only been a means to an end, but Anand admitted to himself that he always did enjoy it. Especially as he knew that more often than not, the truth was far from the stereotype.

7

'How the hell can you not know your own house keys, Amma?'

The men carrying packed cardboard boxes out of the house paused for a moment, taken aback, then continued with their task.

Shakuntala sat on the sofa, alternating between sobbing over Ravi's various possessions being removed from the house and dealing with a livid Charu. 'How can you speak to me like that!' she retorted between sniffles.

Charu took a deep breath, trying to calm down. Between her own discomfort at discarding the remnants of Ravi's life and the fact she knew now that his death was not what they had thought it to be, she struggled to sort out the numerous keys in his desk drawer. Her mother was of no help.

When she had returned home the previous day, Charu had gone straight to her laptop to look up Anand's details. Only when she had found a couple of old newspaper articles, had she felt better about the direction her brother's matter had taken. One of the articles had given a rather detailed résumé of Anand's stellar investigative career, culminating

41

in a medal from the chief minister of the state. Anand at least believed her and he appeared competent enough to find out the truth.

Charu had toyed with the idea of telling Shakuntala about her findings at the police station and her meeting with Anand, but had then decided against it. Not only would it be too much for the poor woman to handle, but Charu certainly did not want the situation at home to be as grim and hopeless as her mood was. Instead, she told Shakuntala that David was helping her close Ravi's bank accounts, find a tenant for the house and deal with the inevitable paperwork required for them to move overseas.

At the mention of David's name, Shakuntala had calmed down and Charu suspected there would be fewer questions now about her comings and goings. She would just have to keep Shakuntala away from this business as far as possible.

'I'm sorry, Amma,' Charu said, sitting down on the sofa next to her mother. 'But this is not easy. And there's much to do.'

At that, Shakuntala wiped her tears away and pulled Charu into a hug. 'My poor baby. To lose your father and your brother at such a young age. It's too much, I know. And it has barely been two weeks . . .'

Charu let Shakuntala sniffle her way to temporary composure as they both watched the volunteers remove the last of the boxes with Ravi's possessions. She had barely shut the door and moved away from it when the doorbell rang. Charu opened the door to find Jitesh standing there, his large frame filling most of the doorway.

'Hi. May I come in?'

'Of course!' Charu admitted him into the living room.

Jitesh walked in. This time he was alone. He said namaste to Shakuntala, then took a seat and indulged in casual enquiries till, as expected, Shakuntala asked him if he would like coffee or tea and left the room to see to the requested beverage.

Jitesh turned to Charu, who sat diagonally across him and said, 'I saw you, yesterday. At Vega Mall. Look, I don't mean to be intrusive or creepy, but it seemed to me that you and David were having an argument. I just wanted to make sure everything was okay. I mean, I've kind of trusted David to help you sort out things here, knowing how close he and your brother were, but if there is any problem . . .'

'No, no problem at all,' Charu said, as she wondered what part of her conversation in the mall could have been construed as an argument. And where had Jitesh seen her anyway, without her noticing his presence?

'Is there anything at all I can help with, Charu?' Jitesh persisted.

Charu frowned, toying for a moment with the idea of telling Jitesh about the investigation, such as it was, that she had commissioned. Being the operations head of a media company, Jitesh was, she noted, a well-connected and influential man and could be of some use.

Maybe, even more useful than David and Anand.

Charu was about to act on the thought when Jitesh spoke again.

'Even if there's nothing I can do to help as such, I was hoping to at least cheer you up with a nice dinner . . . if it's not inappropriate, that is. And if Aunty permits.'

Resisting the urge to give Jitesh a glare at the mention of needing her mother's permission to go out on a date, Charu focused on the invitation. Perhaps an evening out would do her some good. And Jitesh was not a bad prospect on paper. But something about the way he had begun by mentioning an argument ticked Charu off and, as she reminded herself, she was hardly in the prospecting frame of mind. Dinner would have been nice, but she did not know what complications would come with it.

As Charu searched for a polite excuse, Shakuntala came out of the kitchen, carrying three tumblers of coffee on a tray. Charu got up to help, taking the tray from her mother, when her cell phone rang, clattering as it vibrated against the surface of the coffee table.

Charu frowned but said nothing as Shakuntala proprietarily picked up the phone and answered it.

'David! Why didn't you come upstairs when you dropped Charu off yesterday? Yes, yes, I know you must be busy. Thanks for helping her despite that. She doesn't know the city at all and she's just a young girl. Yes, she is here. I'll just give it to her. And make sure you come for dinner today, I will make your favourite onion sambar.' Shakuntala finally held out the phone.

Charu placed the tray on the table and took the phone with a roll of her eyes.

'Hello, young girl,' David's deep voice drawled over the line.

'David, I swear—'

'Ha ha, sorry. I couldn't resist. Anyway, could you come over to my place in a couple of hours, say by 5 p.m.? Anand Uncle says he has some information for us and he prefers not to discuss it in a public place. I suggested we meet here because I didn't think Shakuntala Amma knew about all this. Hope that's okay?'

'Yes, yes, it's fine. Text me the address, please?'

'Will do. Oh, and can you please get the latest copy of Ravi's mobile bill. Anand Uncle asked for it.'

'Sure. Bye.'

Charu disconnected the call as Shakuntala asked her, 'Going out with David?'

'Yes, Amma.' Charu glanced at Jitesh, who sat sipping his coffee. She gave him an apologetic look and added, 'Some . . . paperwork.'

Jitesh smiled at Charu. 'Next time, then?' he softly asked.

Charu nodded. 'Yes, most definitely. In fact,' she added, as a new suspicion crept into her mind, 'does the day after work?'

'I'll make it work.' Setting his now-empty tumbler on the table, Jitesh thanked Shakuntala for the coffee before turning again to Charu. 'I'll call you day after morning to fix a time?'

'Sure.'

'Okay then.'

'Okay. Thanks, Jitesh.'

Charu closed the door on a departing Jitesh and then turned to face a curious—or was it suspecting—Shakuntala.

'He's much older than you are. And divorced too,' Shakuntala said before Charu could speak.

'Amma!'

Shakuntala took Charu's hands in hers. 'You're in a vulnerable state, Charu. It's natural for you to want some . . . support, some hope for the future, a man around the house. Be careful that you don't make hasty decisions.'

Charu bit back a reply that yes, she was hurting and emotional, but that still left her capable of handling herself and the situation and without needing to run in search of the nearest man to take control of things. She took a deep breath. 'All right, Amma. I understand.'

Shakuntala looked pleased with Charu's acquiescence, mistaking it for maturity, which, Charu supposed, it was. There was no point getting into needless arguments on principle alone, a resolution that was severely tested as Shakuntala added, 'Anyway, David is there, no. He will take care of everything.'

'Yes. I should get ready to leave. I need to meet him by five,' Charu said, pulling away from Shakuntala.

'Okay. Take the house keys in case you're late. I'll leave dinner on the table; make sure he eats . . . and you too. By the way, you were trying to figure out keys, no? That one looks like it might fit the front door.'

'I tried it. It doesn't fit anything. But don't worry, I'll figure it out. I better get ready and leave. And Amma . . . sorry again.'

Shakuntala gave Charu a forgiving smile and went into the kitchen. By the time Charu left the house, the smell of onion sambar and roasted potatoes filled the air, as though it were a normal day.

At exactly 5 p.m., Charu rang the doorbell to David's apartment. She had to wait a few moments for the door to open, though the delay was explained at once by David's appearance. He had apparently been in the shower, for his hair was a mess and his T-shirt clung to his still-wet torso. As she caught a whiff of David's shampoo and aftershave, Charu had to remind herself that she had instinctively been both wary of and pissed off with the man. As if to reinforce her initial sentiments, David's smile on seeing her was all too charming. She realized he was far too smooth for her liking, as stereotypical as the bias was.

Add to this, David apologized for a mess that was not, as he invited her in. His flat was new and reeked of money that was inherited and not earned, despite the obvious pretence at a rebellious bachelor lifestyle; the hard rock posters and the framed graffiti art on the walls were but a start. But, Charu noticed, an entire wall of the living room had been given over to a bookshelf filled with titles that were far from easy reads, and more books on a variety of subjects were piled on the coffee table. She would have dismissed the collection as posturing, if not for the lined spines, the dog-eared pages and the occasional bookmarks, ranging from Post-its and bills to beer coasters, that she noticed in some of the books. David was clearly a bunch of contradictions, not all of them unpleasant.

'Tea, coffee or . . . ?'

Charu narrowed her eyes at the hackneyed come-on.

David seemed to have realized she had taken his question as such for he clarified, 'There's wine, but it's cheap. There's cold beer too. I can always call the neighbourhood wine shop if you'd like something else.'

'Beer's fine,' Charu said. David nodded and went to fetch her a can from the fridge as Charu studied his collection of books.

'Here you go . . . *young girl*.' David opened a can and passed it to her, then opened one for himself.

Charu rolled her eyes at him before knocking her can against his, then taking a gulp. She then looked around the simple but stylish apartment, wondering about David's tastes even as she searched for a neutral topic to make conversation about when the doorbell rang.

'That'll be Anand Uncle.' David finished the rest of his beer in a gulp, set the empty can down and wiped his mouth with the back of his hand before moving towards the front door and opening it.

Charu considered the half-drunk beer in her hand, caught between the emphatic need to be herself and the niggling awareness that impressions mattered much in the country she still called home. She was saved from having to decide either way by Anand's cheerful greeting and his immediate request that David get him a cold beer too.

'How was your day?' Anand asked her.

He cleared his throat even before she could think to answer and Charu realized that he was unsure how to start. She also suspected it was not a position Anand often found himself in. A pang of despair settled, heavy, in the pit of her stomach.

'You know something,' she said, the urgency making her words sound harsh. 'What is it? What did you find out?'

Anand sighed and gave David, who stood holding out a beer in an absurd stillness, a look. Anand took the beer; David sat down next to Charu.

Charu waited only long enough to allow Anand to take a swig of his drink before persisting, 'Sir, please . . .'

'Ravi's death was anything but an accident, Charu. And the lorry really had been stolen, I'm guessing, with intent to make the whole thing look like an accident. But it's quite likely that your brother may have been attacked—even killed—before he was placed behind the wheel of his car.'

He paused, waiting for either Charu or David to speak. David was gritting his teeth, as though forcing himself to hold still. Charu's shock showed as a vacant expression. Not knowing what else to say, Anand launched into a brief account of his day, from his discussions with a forensic investigator he knew to his visit to the lorry booking office and then to the site where the lorry had been parked—illegally—for the night and had since been stolen. And then, he had nothing left but silence. He let it hang over them all.

At last, Charu blurted out, 'Ravi was murdered?'

'Most likely, yes.'

'But why?'

'I don't know. That's what we need to find out.'

'By whom?'

'We need to find that out too,' Anand answered, 'at least enough for us to take this back to the police and ask them to reopen the investigation. The evidence I've shared with you is an off-the-record assessment. We'll have to give them due cause to go over the evidence again and see what we see.'

Charu stared at nothing, then, needing to move, took a sip of her beer. She grimaced as she realized it had already gone warm and set the half-empty can on the table. David immediately got up to get more beers, passing them around.

Anand waved his away and said, 'I'd better get going. Do you have Ravi's mobile phone bill? I'll try and look into the phone calls he made and received. See if that gets us anywhere.'

Charu took two sheets of paper out of her bag and handed them over to Anand, who took a cursory look at them.

Anand said, 'The last call Ravi made or received was on the day of the accident, a few minutes past 6 p.m. According to what you told me, David, he had left his office by then.'

David, who was looking at the bill over Anand's shoulder, nodded and said in a strained voice, 'That's my number. I was the last person Ravi talked to.' He moved away and stood looking out of the window as he finished his beer in three large gulps.

Anand gave him a few moments before asking, 'What did you two talk about?'

'Nothing much,' David replied, turning from the window. 'He didn't mention the blood donation. Just said he was bored, sitting in traffic. Asked me about my assignment. We ended up talking about that and some other random work things. Once the traffic started moving, he hung up, saying he didn't have a handsfree set.'

'So whatever went wrong, it had to have happened in the couple of hours since you spoke,' Anand surmised. 'Are you sure everything was all right with him at that point? Ravi did not mention anything out of the ordinary?'

David shrugged as if to say that he either did not know or had not noticed. He picked up another beer, then seemed to think the better of it and put it back in the fridge.

'All right, then.' Anand got up to leave.

David saw him to the door and then told Charu, 'Come, I'll drop you home.'

'But—'

'It's just two beers. And I could do with the drive. There's no way I'm sitting by myself in this house after what we've just heard.'

Charu nodded, acknowledging not only what David had just said but also the fact that the grim truth of the whole situation would not go away even if they stopped talking about it. In a bid to divert herself and David, she joked, 'If you keep dropping me home every day, the neighbours are going to think you're my boyfriend . . . or my driver.'

David considered the statement, apparently in all seriousness. 'Which one would you prefer I was?' he asked. He burst into a loud guffaw at the shocked expression on Charu's face, at which she too joined in, tentative at first and then in wholehearted relief. Still smiling, they both left David's apartment.

8

'What's the matter?' Charu broke the silence between them as she saw David glance into the rearview mirror for the third time in less than ten seconds. She also realized he had been doing that a lot, even though the roads were near-empty in the quiet residential area they were driving through.

'Nothing. It's probably nothing,' David replied.

Charu did not let up, turning in her seat to look behind them. A red van was about twenty metres behind them. Charu watched as David took a turn, then another, and realized what it was that had been bothering him: the other vehicle was clearly following them.

Deciding that panic, not discretion, was the better part of valour, David stepped on the accelerator. It turned out to be the wrong decision; the red van immediately moved with a greater burst of speed. Nearly running them off the narrow road and into a rainwater canal as it overtook them, the van screeched to a halt, barring the way.

David gunned his jeep into reverse but had barely moved a few metres when a bike swerved to a stop right in his path. For a moment, David considered running the man and bike over. Before he could bring himself to take such an extreme step, a man got out of the van and began to walk towards them.

Charu acted at once, reaching over to make sure the windows were up and the doors were locked.

The man stopped in his tracks.

Charu and David let out sighs of relief, though with some disbelief—and rightly so.

The man walked back to his vehicle, opened the trunk and pulled out a metal rod before coming towards them again.

'Fuck!' David made to step on the accelerator again, meaning to run over the man on the bike, consequences be damned, but before he could, the man with the metal pipe brought the instrument down with a precise blow, cracking open the cover to the petrol tank.

'What is he doing?' Charu exclaimed, though the answer soon became apparent.

The assailant took out a length of cloth from his pocket and stuffed one end into the open petrol tank. Pulling out a lighter with his other hand, he flicked it on and gave David and Charu a meaningful look.

'Don't. It's a bluff. If he lights the tank he'll get blown up too,' Charu said.

The man seemed to have heard them. With a shake of his head, he picked up the edge of the cloth dangling out of the petrol tank and began moving backwards till he was at the very edge of the road and stood right next to the rainwater canal—and the cover it would provide. The man on the motorcycle too revved up his vehicle and moved a few metres away.

'Charu—'

'No, David.'

The man brought the lighter's flame to the edge of the cloth, setting it alight.

Charu and David scrambled out of the jeep as the man with the lighter pulled the cloth out from the petrol tank, stamping on the lit edge to put out the flame. Then, before David and Charu could think of escaping, the accomplice on the motorbike and he closed in on them. The man with the lighter—clearly the leader of the two—put it back into his pocket and used both hands to grab David and pin him against the jeep. He then signalled to his accomplice, who grabbed Charu by the hair and dragged her a few feet away before forcing her to her knees, in full view of David. The threat having been made, the leader then turned his attention back to David.

'*Maal kuthe re*?' Where's the money?

'What?' David gasped out the question before the thug lay on to him, first with a punch to his face and then another one to the stomach that had David doubling over. Making good on the chance, the man grabbed David's arm and twisted it behind his back, making David scream in pain. Finally, he yanked David up by the back of his T-shirt and slammed him back against the jeep.

'David! No, please! Don't hurt him!' Charu began pleading at the sight. David could hardly stand; blood dribbled out of his mouth.

The lead thug ignored her, again asking David, 'Money. I want the money.'

More blood spurted out as David opened his mouth. Nevertheless, he tried to speak, mumbling something that the thug could not make sense of.

'Playing games, huh?' The man decided that David needed more motivation. He picked up the metal rod from where he had thrown it on the ground.

'No! Stop! I have money. I'll give it to you. Please don't hurt him!' Charu cried out.

'Eh?' The thug turned around, surprised and pleased at the sudden turn of events. 'You have the money?'

Charu was frantic. 'I do. I do. It's in the car. Please, take it all, take everything. Don't hurt him, please.'

The lead thug waved to his accomplice, who then pulled Charu to her feet. Still gripping her by her hair, he led her around the jeep, to the passenger side. A watchful eye on Charu all the while, he held her back and opened the door. 'Where is it?'

Charu pointed at her bag. 'Please,' she added, 'Please don't hurt us. I'll give you everything.'

She tremulously reached for her handbag. The thug tightened his grip on her hair in a silent reminder to not try anything funny. Curling her fingers around the strap, she pulled the bag towards her and then passed it behind to the waiting man.

The grip on her hair eased as the thug prepared to look into the bag.

Charu acted, throwing herself stomach down across the seats to press down on the car's horn, even as she kicked out blindly at her attacker, hoping to get him off her.

Many things happened at once. The lead thug, realizing that Charu had tricked him, brought up the iron rod and used it to choke David by pressing it down on his neck while he was still pinned. Charu, however, could not see the added danger David was in and kept her fist punched down on the horn. The second thug, having momentarily reeled back from Charu's kick, now came at her, grabbing her by her hair and her kurti, trying to pull her out of the car. Charu grabbed the door handle on the driver's side with her other hand and held on with all her might.

Lights came on in the surrounding apartments as people emerged on their balconies to investigate—and curse at—the incessant honking. A few security guards emerged from their respective buildings. One of them caught sight of the scene and shouted out a warning to his colleagues. A whistle started blowing as the security guards sounded the alarm. Within seconds, the whistle had attracted the attention of a solitary police car on its usual rounds and the sound of a siren was soon heard in the distance.

With the odds now against them, the thugs had no choice but to beat a hasty retreat. Leaving the bike where it was, the two men ran towards their van.

The moment the man took his hands off her, Charu slid out of the jeep and made her way to where David was slumped on to the ground.

'David! David!'

'He's not dead. Not yet. Listen, asshole! You have four days to give us our money. Otherwise we'll hurt your girlfriend here next. We'll be watching her,' the lead thug called out to her as he zipped past, forcing a security guard to jump out of the way.

Four days? Our money?

The words made no sense to Charu, but she thought of them no further as David coughed up more blood. His chest heaved, but then he opened his eyes, now swollen into slits, to look up at Charu.

'Never knew . . . being your driver . . . such a dangerous job. Thank . . . thank god I'm not your boyfriend,' he said, in an attempt at a joke.

As relief, the depths of which she had not expected, filled Charu, there was only one thing she could say. 'Don't be fucking silly.'

9

Anand found Charu in the mosquito-infested courtyard outside the emergency room at the General Hospital. She was on the phone, clearly with her mother on the other end, from the way she kept trying to argue that both she and David were fine. She hung up as he approached, with a 'Don't worry, Amma! It was just a small accident. Now, bye!' and greeted him with a smile.

'Are you okay?' Anand asked her without prelude.

'Yes.'

'And David?'

'Fine. Thankfully all the blood he was spitting out was from a broken tooth and not internal injuries.' She added, 'He's alternating between making bad jokes and telling the nurses that he has done amateur boxing, so these injuries are nothing to him.'

Anand laughed softly. He said, 'You must have been pretty shook up. Did they hit you too?'

'I was a bit shook up, yeah. And it was nothing. I'm okay now . . .'

'But?'

'Hmm?'

Anand gave her a telling look. 'From what you told me on the phone, this wasn't just a random robbery. Those guys were looking specifically for money they thought you had. And they've given you four days to rustle it up. Correct?'

'Not money I had, Anand sir. Money that they thought David had. *Their* money. I didn't realize that, which is why I tried to give them what I had in my handbag. But now that I think back to everything those guys said and did . . . it was David they were after. Which makes me wonder . . .' Charu trailed off, casting a part-anxious, part-doubtful look in the direction of the emergency room.

Anand was gentle but unwavering. 'Do you think he had something to do with your brother's death? Or that this money thing is somehow connected?'

Charu shook her head. 'No. I don't think so. I mean, I'm not sure what I think, sir.'

'You suspect him of something, even if you're not sure exactly what, correct?'

'Yes.'

Anand laughed and said, 'You know me only through David. And though you met him for the first time just a few days ago, the fact remains that he has known your family for over three years now; he was your brother's best friend. Yet, you are willing to trust me more than you trust him, to the point that you admit you suspect him. Why is that?'

Charu shrugged. 'I would say it's instinct, but that would be irrational. The truth is, I looked you up—your record in the police force, your family—I know more about you than I do about David.' She then shook her head and added, 'I don't know, sir. He's my brother's best friend. My mother adores him. But . . . but he makes me feel as though I don't know what he's really thinking. And just when I thought I was being overcritical and was beginning to think he's a nice man, that we could be friends, this happens.'

Anand thought for a moment then said, 'That's true. It's tough to tell what David's thinking. He's very good at keeping up an unflappable façade. But that's just how he is. I've known him since he was just a boy. You're aware of that, right? Well, call me biased, but I've seen him turn out okay over the years.'

He explained as Charu gave him a questioning look, 'David's mom died when he was a kid. His father was a very strict man and gave David the hardest time . . . often with his belt. Of course, it's not like the boy wasn't up to all sorts of mischief. There was a point, in fact, after he got thrown out of school for the fourth time that I almost gave up on him. I thought he was a lost cause. But still, I used my contacts to get him into another school. I don't know if running out of chances had anything to do with it, or maybe he just found the right kind of friends, but he turned himself around, pulled his grades up to above average and started playing sports. He was quite a popular guy in college, from what I know. But I always suspected that being the cool, funny guy, the "I don't give a damn" act, was David's way of dealing with the fact that he could never please his father. Nothing he did was ever good enough. When Daniel died, about seven years ago, he and David were not on talking terms.'

Charu considered the words with a frown. 'So David has problems. Who doesn't?'

'Charu—'

'Sir, are you telling me David is totally clean? That this whole incident really is just an attempted theft?'

'I'm a policeman, Charu. I don't think anybody is innocent of a crime unless someone is found indisputably guilty. I'd suspect even you, if the cause arose. As for whether David is clean . . .' Anand snorted. 'No one is ever fully clean or perfectly good. At least, not if they've had the opportunity.'

Anand finished with a non-committal shrug that he suspected left Charu more confused than comforted. She was clearly worried, not just about the incident with the thugs in itself, but at the prospect of David having been hurt. While some concern was undoubtedly born of human decency, there was something about Charu's expression that Anand could not fathom.

He was about to comment on it when David, part of his face and all of his left forearm in bandages, hobbled out of the emergency area and up to where they stood.

'David! Can you walk?' Anand asked him, letting the other matter go for the moment.

'Yeah, Uncle. I'm just tired. My legs aren't hurt in the least.'

'Let me drop you both home.'

'Thanks.'

Charu, who had driven herself and David to the hospital, handed David's car key to Anand and said, 'It's all right, sir. I'll just take a taxi home.' She began walking off without waiting for a response.

To her surprise, there was none. David did not try to stop her. He did not say anything at all. Turning to Anand, he took his car key with a mumbled thanks and left.

Anand watched him go, wondering if he should remind the younger man that driving home with his arm in a bandage and under the influence of painkillers was not the best thing to do. He decided against it; he had something else on his mind.

Money.

And likely, a good deal of money. Loan sharks and thugs had been known to hurt, even kill, over a few thousand rupees, but that was often a matter of protecting their reputation than it was about getting their payment. In this case, given the level of discretion, if it could be called that, the thugs had shown suggested they were more interested in making sure the money was returned. Whatever the sum was, Anand knew, it could not be a negligible one, not if it merited the cost and effort of recovery.

Anand smiled to himself as he flagged down a waiting taxi. Money always made things interesting. In more ways than one.

10

David waited till he was home and the door firmly shut behind him before he let himself drop to his knees. He let his head sink to the floor, his mouth open in a silent scream as he let out all that he had been holding back for weeks now, including the tears he had refused to shed for Ravi, firstly because he had been in the wrong place and far from alone, and then because it had been too late for crying to make sense any more.

By the time he had returned to Mumbai, David had thought he had made peace with the loss, in some fashion or the other. He reasoned that he could, he would, move on, even though Ravi had been the only family he had had. The void would remain, nothing would be the same and his life would be many shades duller after this, but he would go on.

And then, Charu had blazed into existence, tearing apart his self-set equanimity.

Is it wrong that I feel happy around her? Is it wrong that I want to feel happy so soon?

Despite Shakuntala's many suggestions over the years that David and Charu might 'get along well', as she had put it, David had always laughed the idea off. His best friend's sister did not have to be a sister to him, but in his book, she was off limits. Besides, what sense would it make to get a nice girl involved with a man like him, with his own messed-up affairs?

And so, when Ravi had talked at length, as he often did, about his little sister and how she made him proud, what an intelligent, strong-willed girl she was, David had simply listened and shared in Ravi's joy, never for a moment thinking of Charu as anything beyond a topic of conversation, not even as a person, really.

As for the Charu he had spent most of the past two days with, the Charu who had taken his breath away even as he had first seen her, crouched in faded Mickey Mouse pyjamas over a pile of garbage . . . it still did not matter. His life was still too much of a mess for him to want her to be a part of it, no matter how strong a person she was. Besides, he supposed, it was a little too late for even wanting that, after what had happened last night.

Charu, David knew, would have easily figured out that the goons had meant to target him and that there was more to that story. *Is it even worth trying to explain to her who they are and what I am caught up in?*

No. She had enough problems of her own, and he was already adding to them. Maybe he should not have offered to help with looking into Ravi's death. Maybe he should not have brought Anand in to investigate. But God, at that moment there had been nothing more he had wanted than to lay the world at Charu's feet, stupid as that sounded.

Love is overrated, Ravi would sometimes say when they drank together on weekends. *You're wasting your time waiting for love, David. You are hot property. Make the most of it. We shall live fast and die young, my friend.*

Well, one of them had managed to get one part of that right.

Pulling himself to his feet, David made his way to the kitchen, where he took off his bloodstained T-shirt and threw it in the garbage bin. Then, uncaring of the fact that it was barely an hour or so to sunrise, he grabbed a bottle of rum from a cupboard and began drinking straight from it. By the time dawn broke, he had fallen into a restless sleep, sprawled on the sofa, the empty bottle of rum next to him.

'Fuck!' The incessant buzzing of the doorbell brought David out of his drunken stupor.

'Fuck! Fuck! Fuck!' He cursed again as he realized, in order, that it was four in the afternoon and he had slept through the day, that his head throbbed from the combined effects of the rum and the goon's fist, and finally, that he reeked of alcohol and was in no state to admit whoever it was at the door. Nevertheless, as the visitor showed no signs of relenting, he stumbled across the room to the door and opened it. It was Charu, bearing an inscrutable expression on her face and a tiffin carrier in her hand.

She walked into the house without a word. David hesitantly shut the door behind her. Charu made her way over to the dining table and began setting out the food. David stood around uncertainly till she turned around and said, 'Go brush your teeth, then come eat. Anand Uncle will be coming around in a while.'

By the time David had freshened up—going one step further to shower and get into clean clothes—Charu had settled herself on the sofa with a copy of *The Adventures of Sherlock Holmes*, a new copy of one of his childhood favourites, from his shelf. She did not look up as he emerged and left him to eat on his own. David forced down what he could of Shakuntala's delicious cooking despite his lack of appetite. He cleared away the rest, making more of a mess as he tried to carry many things using his bandaged arm. When he was done, he looked around for the packet of medicines the doctors at the emergency room had equipped him with.

'It's on the kitchen counter. You must have put it there when you took the rum out,' Charu said.

David looked up to see that she had set the book aside and was watching him. He cleared his throat as he searched for something to say, then settled on telling her, 'You can borrow the book, if you like.'

Charu considered the book as though she were about to throw it across the room at David, but then slid the volume into her bag and stared into space. David realized this was not going to be easy, after all.

I guess I totally deserve this.

He came up to her, crouched down to bring himself eye to eye with her, and said, 'Charu, please. I can explain—'

'Go take your medicines, David. I'm sure that arm still hurts.'

'Charu—'

'Anand sir will be here soon, David. I need you to have a clear head when he does. Please go take your medicines.'

Sighing at her stubbornness—or was it anger—David did as he was told. He was in the kitchen when the doorbell rang. He could hear Charu get up to open the door, the muted conversation as she let Anand in. David flinched as he heard Anand say, 'Have you asked him yet?' Charu's response was a mumble that he could not catch. Trying to stuff the many emotions he felt into whatever distinct compartments he could, David stepped out of the kitchen.

Charu wasted no time. 'Why did you lie to me, David?'

'What do you mean, Charu? About those guys last night . . . I can explain.'

'It's more than that, David, and you know it.'

'I—I really . . .' A floundering David looked from Charu to Anand, as though pleading for the latter to help.

Anand was sympathetic but unyielding as he said, 'I made some enquiries in the area around Ravi's office building today, David. You two were seen arguing in public the day he died. One of the security guards told me. In fact, you came to blows, pushing each other around, grabbing each other by the collar and such.'

David stared at Anand for a moment, then collapsed into one of the single-seater sofas.

Charu went up and crouched down in front of him, as he had just a short while ago. 'You said nothing to us about this argument, David; about the goons and the money. You and Ravi were at each other's throats the day he died but still you . . . you acted as if everything was fine. You lied, you pretended to be puzzled and shocked by his death. You tricked us, David. You tricked *me*. Why?'

David met her gaze, his eyes full of anger, pain and self-loathing. 'Because it's my fault, Charu. It's my fault that Ravi is dead.'

Neither the dramatic declaration nor its attendant guilt had an effect on Charu and Anand. They both waited for David to continue.

David began in a resigned monotone, 'The day before he died, Ravi approached me, asking if I could help him get forty lakh rupees. He said he was in deep trouble, and he needed it by the next day. I tried, I tried my best, I emptied out my bank account, I borrowed from whomever I could. But I couldn't scrape together much.'

He looked up at Anand, 'That's what we fought about. Ravi was livid that I hadn't arranged all the money for him. He said he'd be dead by the evening if he didn't show up with the whole amount. I asked him what the fuck he had done to put himself in such a position; what was going on. He said it was none of my business. He—he accused me of having more money but not giving it to him. That's when we—we shoved each other around a bit. Then, I got pissed off and left. Maybe if I hadn't, maybe if I'd just stuck around . . .'

Charu asked, 'What happened that evening? You were the last person to speak to him, David. What did he *really* say?'

David turned his gaze to Charu, 'He said the whole thing had been sorted out, that he had managed the rest of the money and everything was going to be okay. I—I really should have stayed. I should have gone with him . . . wherever it was he was going.'

'You might be dead too if you'd done that. At least now we have something to go on,' Anand said. 'So, there are two options here: First, that Ravi might have been killed by those he owed the money to. But that doesn't hold up; thugs don't kill those who owe them money till they've got their hands on it, because they may not have a way of getting it once their mark is dead. And we know that they still don't have the cash because they came after you two.'

'Could Ravi have been killed for the money?' Charu asked. 'I mean by someone who knew he had so much cash and wanted to steal it? But no, that doesn't make sense either. It was too short a timeframe for someone to plan such a thing. And it can't have been a random mugging. A robber like that would not go to the extent of faking an accident to cover up the murder.'

'Correct,' Anand said. 'Which leaves us with option two . . . option three actually, given that we are also ruling out a random robbery. Ravi was killed because of whatever trouble he had got himself into. His death was not so much about the money as it was about what he had done.

We'll get more information by tomorrow on the other calls he made and received that day. Let's take it from there.'

David did not shift his gaze from Charu. 'I'm sorry, Charu.'

Charu stood up. '"Sorry", David? I trusted you, and you hid things from me; you lied to me. "Sorry" is supposed to fix all that?'

David sprang to his feet, towering over her as he spit out, 'So what the fuck was I supposed to do? Tell you and your mother that Ravi wasn't the clean, nice guy you thought he was? That he was deep in shit from doing god knows what? For heaven's sake, I've been scrambling around, trying to arrange forty lakh to get those guys off my back . . . and yours. They threatened you because they thought you were my girlfriend. How long do you think it will take them to figure out that you're Ravi's sister and to come after you—or Amma—with a vengeance? And this is what I get?'

'Thank you for protecting us,' Charu replied with sarcasm. 'I'm sure Ravi is very grateful for it.'

'Charu—'

Without another word, Charu turned around and left, closing the front door hard in her rage.

David went after her. 'Charu, please—'

But she had already got into the lift and the doors had closed.

David stood in the corridor, deliberating whether he ought to follow her downstairs, even go to her house to try and talk to her.

'My advice? Give her time,' Anand said, coming up to stand beside him and calling up the lift. 'You did lie to us, David. If this were an actual police investigation, what you did would have been seen as deliberately impeding an investigation. It would have been a crime.'

'I'm sorry, Uncle. I mean it. I was just trying to—'

'Get some rest, my boy.'

David waited till the lift doors had closed again, then made his way back into the house. He headed straight into the kitchen in search of yet another bottle. He finished the half-full bottle of vodka he found in a matter of minutes and then telephoned the bar nearby to ask them to deliver more. Within a matter of hours, David had passed out in a restless sleep.

11

'Did he eat? How is he feeling?'

Charu had to grit her teeth to not shout in response to Shakuntala's concerned questions the moment she entered the house. She simply said, 'Yes, Amma. He's better. Just needs rest.'

Shakuntala appeared satisfied with the answer, for she then turned her attention to plying Charu with dinner. She then cleared things away and retired for the night, but not without a caution. 'Don't stay up too long, Charu. You need to rest too, *kanna*.'

Charu nodded and watched her go, staring at what she was already aware of but really noticed for the first time as Shakuntala had served her dinner: the gleaming gold bangles on her mother's hands. She remembered the excited video call when her mother had alternated between childlike joy and equally childlike tears at the bangles Ravi had bought her, saying it was the first time she had worn new jewellery since their father had died. It had never occurred to Charu then to ask where Ravi had got the money from. That cluster of bangles was worth at least a couple of lakhs, maybe more.

Charu waited till her mother was inside the room, then began looking around the living area she stood in, taking in the large-screen TV and the new stereo system. Ravi had even bought Charu a new state-of-the-art laptop when he and their mother had visited her in the US. Charu had tried to talk him out of it, arguing that their trip itself must have set him back a hefty sum, but Ravi had not been dissuaded. He also had, Charu remembered, bought a fairly high-end laptop for himself. *Had he been borrowing money? Or was it something more complicated? Where has all this stuff come from?* Sure, Ravi was doing well at work, but it was hardly a CEO's job, and she had expected much of his savings to have gone towards their mother's medical treatments. Shakuntala had a host of niggling issues, ranging from diabetes to hypertension, and Ravi had made sure that she got the best medicines available in the market to deal with her condition. *How had he managed it all?* Perhaps, she told herself, David was telling the truth after all. But how was she to make sure of that?

Ravi's laptop was missing; either stolen from the site of the accident or lost during the investigation. In any case, the police claimed that they had not found his laptop in the car. But there was another way to find out more about Ravi and his online activities.

Going into her room—Ravi's room—Charu pulled out her laptop and accessed the modem's server in the house, pulling up the search history against the IP address of their home network. Ignoring her mother's injunction to get some rest, Charu set herself to going through the Internet history with a vengeance.

It took much longer and required far more digging than Charu had expected for something to catch her eye. About a year and a half ago, Ravi had searched for private locker rentals in Mumbai and even visited some of the websites that the search had thrown up. The finding jogged a memory into place and Charu's hand dived into the desk drawer, where she had thrown the jumbled bunch of unidentified keys she had collected while going through Ravi's stuff. She pulled out the fancy-looking laser-cut key.

'Shit! Now, what would *you* want with a security locker, Ravi? That too a private one?'

The key clenched in her fist as though it gave her new energy, Charu began going through the website links. For a moment, she thought she might have to set Anand on the task; most of the facilities she found were in the Fort area. Then she happened upon SafeCo, a professional-looking but barebones website informing her that their only high-security branch was located not too far, by Mumbai standards at least, from Ravi's office. She also noticed that SafeCo appeared to be open late into the night. 11 p.m., as the time now showed, could be deemed early by their standards.

Charu stowed the laser-cut key inside a zippered compartment of her bag and sneaked out of the house, careful not to wake Shakuntala up. She headed downstairs to a nearby taxi stand, managing after some time to find a taxi driver who would ply her for one-and-a-half times the meter rate, given the late hour. As she bundled herself into the taxi, Charu thought about calling David and dialled his number once pragmatism overtook her anger. There was no response. She tried a few more times before giving up, even as a niggling sense of guilt crept up on her. Yes, he had lied to her, but then, as he had said, how was he to tell her that there was more to her doting gentleman of a brother than she had known. She did not, however, have the chance to dwell on the matter for long; the taxi turned into a dimly lit street with a few shops—all of them now shut—and came to a stop.

Charu peered out the cab window, taking in the deserted street, the faint reek of urine and garbage a far cry from the more sophisticated surroundings she had expected of SafeCo. But as the sole lit-up board on the street declared, this was indeed where she had wanted to go.

'Bhaiyya, will you wait? It will take just ten minutes . . .' she asked the driver.

He began to say 'no', but after a look at the surroundings, changed his mind. Nevertheless, not to let an opportunity pass by, no matter his sense of humanity, he said, 'Double meter *lagega*, madam.'

'No problem,' Charu said. Getting out of the taxi, she made her way across the narrow street to SafeCo.

The inside of SafeCo was well-matched to its exteriors. A small room served as the reception, yellow paint peeling off its walls. From a corner hung a cobweb-covered security camera, the wire cut and hanging loose in a clear indication of it being defunct. A young man, hardly seventeen or eighteen years old, snoozed in a plastic wicker chair behind a mica-covered table. A phone and some dog-eared ledgers were the only things on the table, as though this were a bigger-than-usual public phone booth.

Charu knocked on the table, waking up the snoozing man. He yawned, stretched, then sat forward with a bored expression that came of being no stranger to this routine.

'Number?' he asked her, holding out his hand.

Charu was taken aback, but then quickly figured it out. Pulling out the key from her bag, she tried to read the minuscule numbers engraved on it.

The man, apparently used to his clients' myopic ineptitude, said tonelessly: 'Give it here.'

He took the key from Charu, read the number with ease and then pulled out a corresponding ledger from the stacks around him. Opening it to an assigned page, he shoved the ledger towards Charu. 'Sign here,' he said, tapping on the ledger.

Charu did as she was told, but not before taking a moment to note that there were multiple entries against the said locker before hers, all with Ravi's signature against them. The last entry was dated the day before his death.

Charu suddenly felt afraid, but also a strange anticipation at the thought that she might soon know what had happened, why her brother had died. Forcing herself to remain outwardly calm, she signed on the register and waited.

The receptionist—such as he was—eased himself out of the chair and beckoned her to follow as they made their way towards the back of the room and to an aluminum door. Charu walked through the door to find herself in a corridor, the width of which was taken up by an X-ray scanner. The equipment made no noise as she passed through it and Charu could not tell whether it was just another piece of junk like the camera outside. But as they moved through the corridor towards another door at the end of it—this one solid iron, as the door to a safety vault ought to be—the faint telltale smell of air-conditioning wafted towards them. Charu realized that the shoddy exterior was for show—and thereby misdirection. The service SafeCo provided was not only to ensure the safety of their lockers' contents, but also complete discretion—even secrecy—in the use of their facilities.

The thought of what Ravi might have stored in such a place added to the sinking feeling in Charu's stomach.

The receptionist stopped in front of the metal door and fished out a key that was tucked inside his underwear. He used the key, not to open the door but to unlock a small box made of similar reinforced metal to reveal a much-used push-button keypad within. The man punched in a series of numbers with a speed that ensured no observer could make them out. With a clang of metal as heavy-duty bolts shot back, the door opened.

The man stepped aside and waved Charu in. He leaned in briefly to point to a switch. 'Press this when you are finished. I'll come and get you. Your locker is in the stacks on the right.'

Before Charu could say anything, he pulled the vault door shut and was gone.

A stunned Charu took in the sight before her: a carpeted, air-conditioned room; windowless but brightly lit, like a corporate office. In it, stacks and stacks of gleaming metal lockers, each stack bolted securely to both ceiling and floor. Even as Charu wondered how something like this had been left in the care of an anorexic, insipid kid, she realized that the receptionist was a front too. No doubt, there were cameras that actually worked, though they were not meant to be seen, and a team of actual security guards—or goons—watched every arrival and departure, on alert to mobilize at a moment's notice.

Charu found the weirdness of it all quite fitting, given the events of the past few days. Without thinking too much about it, she made her way to a stack of lockers to her right.

The lockers were arranged by numbers and it was not too difficult for Charu to find Ravi's. She inserted her key, took a deep breath and turned it. A part of her hoped that the key would not fit, while another part of her feared that it would not.

The door swung open noiselessly. Charu heaved a sigh of relief as she took in the contents of the locker: a Ziplock bag holding an external hard drive. She grabbed it and stuffed it into the depths of her bag and was about to slam the door shut when she gave in to the thought that the locker was an inordinately large one for Ravi to store just a hard drive. Pulling out her cell phone, Charu switched on the flashlight and shone it into the depths of the locker. Something flashed, almost invisible in the darkness. Charu put her hand inside, reaching into the back of the locker.

Her hands felt canvas; she used her fingers to grab the fabric and tweak the thing forward, realizing quickly that it was a plain, black duffel bag.

She pulled the bag out of the locker and set it on the floor. For no reason that she could fathom or explain, she looked around her, making sure she was alone in the room. Kneeling, Charu unzipped the bag open.

'Oh fuck!' she swore. 'Oh fuck, Ravi. What have you done?'

12

It was true, Charu noted. Money did have its own smell.

It did not occur to her that the thought was a strange one to have at that moment; 'strange' and 'not normal' no longer had their old meanings, not after this. She stared at the contents of the bag, trying, ineffectively, to estimate their value by counting the stacks. As the thousands added up to lakhs and then tens of lakhs, she gave up, pegging the number in her head simply as 'a shitload of money'. A shitload of money that her brother, Ravi, had stowed away.

The same shitload of money that the goons were after.

Charu looked around the room as though the men might just jump out at her from behind the stacks of lockers. It would, she supposed, be a relief in a way to have the matter over and done with and go back to life as it was.

She also knew that her life would never be the same again, not after what Ravi had done.

Ravi.

Coming out of her daze at that, Charu reminded herself that whatever it was her brother had been mixed up in, it did not justify his murder; nothing did. She owed it to him to get to the bottom of that mess, even if the mess had been of his own making.

Charu resolutely zipped the bag close and thrust it back into the depths of the locker. She tucked the hard drive safely inside her handbag and, locking up, made her way out.

The clerk did not give her a second glance as he came to let her out and guided her back to the reception.

Stepping out of the premises, Charu looked around for her taxi. The driver, thankfully, was waiting as promised, though he kept glancing warily up and down the street as though he would be more relieved than her to get out of there. She tipped him over and above the agreed double fare once she reached home, but his unenthusiastic reaction showed he did not deem it enough recompense for his troubles, after all.

Not wanting to get into a haggling match, Charu disappeared into her apartment building. Fortunately, Shakuntala was still asleep as Charu let herself into the house and made her way into her room.

Only when the door closed behind did Charu realize how stiff her neck and shoulders were, how tense her entire body was. She let her bag drop to the ground and then let her body follow suit, sliding down against the closed door to sit on the floor. She wanted to cry, though she did not know why or what for. She also wanted to scream and that she knew well what for: *Why, Ravi? What have you done?*

At that, she remembered the hard drive. Getting up, Charu sat down in front of her laptop and plugged the device in. The drive contained a single folder, inside which were twenty-odd video files. The filenames were self-explanatory: a person's name and a ten-digit number that followed by an underscore character, ostensibly a mobile number.

Charu played a video at random and an orgasmic moan filled the room. She hit pause. She glanced at the door and waited, making sure that Shakuntala had not woken up and was coming to investigate. Reassured, Charu pressed the mute button on her laptop before resuming the video.

It was not porn, not even by amateurish standards. In addition, the video self-adjusted for lack of light, suggesting it was shot with something akin to a CCTV camera. But the contents of the video were clear enough: in what looked like an upscale hotel room, a middle-aged man and a young, attractive woman were engaged in loud, demonstrative sex.

The video ran for a little under three minutes, clearly edited from a longer clip to focus on salient events. Charu then clicked on the second file: similar hotel room, possibly even the same one. A different middle-aged man and a different young woman. But the gist of it was the same. This clip, Charu noted, was a combination of two sequences from the original footage, edited not only to show what was transpiring in the room but also to emphatically capture the face of the gentleman involved in the proceedings.

Charu skimmed through the rest of the videos. There were twenty-six clips, all of three minutes or under. Looking up the system information related to the drive, she realized it had been created using a mirroring software that had copied all contents from a folder on another system, presumably a computer. She ran a recovery protocol on the drive, trying to discover any hidden files or other data she could access. She found over fifty video files, all much larger in size than the first ones and with default filenames in a date-time format. Charu played one of the recovered videos and saw nothing but an empty room. She also noted that the video ran for over fourteen hours. Presumably, these files were raw footage from which the smaller clips had been created.

The discovery left no doubt in Charu's mind that the purpose of the videos was not titillation. They also left a mix of fear and revulsion in the pit of her stomach. Bad taste in porn was something she could have easily forgiven Ravi for. But this was something far more sinister, though she did not dare put a name to it.

Perhaps it was part of an investigation he was doing? Charu tried to defend Ravi to herself. After all, her brother was a reporter. Jitesh would know . . . or would he? Had Ravi, ambitious as he was, been trying to gather a scoop, maybe expose a prostitution racket? But really, in the larger scheme of affairs, this was more sensational reporting than it was investigative and not at all the kind of story her brother would have been interested in.

Or was it? And what about the money? If Ravi did have so much money, why had he not paid off the goons? Or had he borrowed the money to pay them off and that was the cash she had found?

Charu pressed at her temples as she felt the beginnings of a throbbing headache. She had always thought that she knew her brother, that she understood him. She had assumed that they were closer than most siblings, but she now realized that it had been an indulgent, one-way relationship, where Ravi had always been there for her and she had only ever been his little sister. Had she known her brother at all?

The confusion was too much to take and Charu was grateful for the unbidden tears that blurred her vision to the video playing on the screen. *Stop thinking so much!* she told herself. This was Ravi, the boy who had given up on his dreams to make sure she could follow her own. The man who had worked hard to create a career for himself for no reason other than to care of his mother and sister. Ravi was—had been—a good man, a great brother and a decent journalist. The whole affair, disgusting as it was, must have been part of something investigative, something honest and right.

Hanging on to the mild reassurance the possibility gave her, Charu shut down her computer. She took a quick shower, her mind needing it more than her body, and then tucked herself into bed. She tried to lie awake and sift through all that had just happened, all that she had seen. But tired from her day, sleep came as a blessing sooner than she hoped for. Thankfully, Charu did not dream.

13

The sun had risen on the city, but trapped as it was behind the array of skyscrapers, all it could do was give off a diffused light that filtered through the smog to fill the lanes of Anand's residential colony with a countryside-like mist. The illusion lasted only so long and Anand started as a horn blared behind him. He jumped out of the way of a black Pajero driven by a young man who was returning home after a night of revelry, no doubt funded by the considerable fortune his retired policeman father had made in bribes.

Was it worse then? Or is it worse now?

Sensing that he was about to go into a spiral of thoughts too early in the day, Anand shook his head and resumed his brisk morning walk to head home. But, he decided, as he pulled out the curled newspaper that had been tucked into the railings of the small gate and perused the headlines, it was going to be that kind of a day, after all.

MURDER AT PALM GROVE

The news item had, with its immediacy, displaced articles on increasing inflation and a recent spate of farmer suicides to small boxes along the edges of the front page. Below the salacious headline was a picture, strategically blurred, of a decomposing cadaver being wheeled along in a hospital corridor, taken with a long-distance zoom lens. Anand sighed, wondering again how much some morgue attendant had been paid to wheel the body along uncovered so that the nation could get its morning fix of gory. Next to the unauthorized photograph was an unflattering reminder of the man who had once been, posing outside said Palm Grove, a high-end beach resort on the outskirts of the city.

Anand skimmed through the story: Mahesh, as the deceased was identified, had been found dead. His body had washed up in one of the suburban creeks three days ago. The article added that Mahesh had been reported missing about a week ago by his wife, but the initial autopsy indicated that he had been dead for over two weeks.

'Good morning, Uncle! Lovely weather today, no?'

Anand looked up as Naina stepped out of her apartment block, dressed for her morning jog.

'Good morning, Naina,' Anand replied. He held up the newspaper inquiringly.

Naina laughed and nodded. She then walked over, saying, 'Yes, this was the case I was telling you about. We found the missing persons' report buried under a mountain of papers that were awaiting entry into the online database. So much for technology, huh! Like you said, it's still good old-fashioned police work that gets things done.'

Anand smiled and said, 'Well done, *beta*. So, what is it all about?'

'Cause of death was a bullet to the brain from a desi revolver. He'd been beaten up before that. You know what that means, Uncle. Most probably a gang rivalry of some sort. Of course, since there's little the police can do, or even wants to do about it, the official line we've . . . umm . . . *encouraged* journalists to take is that Mahesh was killed as a result of a family dispute because of ongoing tension between his wife and his girlfriend. Makes for a spicier story in any case.'

'Hmm.' Anand looked down at the newspaper again. He could not place it, but something about the murder niggled at him. 'Two weeks ago?' he asked.

'Almost three. Of course, the exact date and time of death are difficult to judge in this case. But I place it at twenty days.'

Which would make it the day before Ravi was killed.

Anand knew from years of experience that murder, horrible as it was, was not all that rare. Even assuming that both murders had occurred on consecutive days, there was nothing to suggest they were related. Indeed, it made the case for them being unrelated. But Anand also knew from those same years of experience that instinct was often just the name given to something the mind had already picked up, but not fully processed into concrete thought. And when it came to solving crime, instinct was not to be ignored.

~

Charu paid the taxi driver and then stood taking in her intended destination in the upper-middle-class area of

Chembur. The semi-detached house was old but well-maintained. Red tiles over the porch, flowering roses in many colours and the white rice-flour lines of a *kolam* on the still-wet area in front of the gate were all familiar from another time, though she had not thought anyone could still afford the idyllic life of her childhood in current times. Strains of 'Sri Venkateswara Suprabhatam'—mandatorily in the voice of M.S. Subbulakshmi—floated out from the open front door along with the smell of incense.

The perfection made her hesitate; surely this did not make sense. Her hand clenched around the rolled-up newspaper in her hand. She did not have to look at it to remember the headline or all that had followed and instead, tucked the newspaper into her bag and out of sight. She then let herself in through the gate and made her way to the open door.

The smell of filter coffee came invitingly as she rang the bell.

'Coming! Coming!' A middle-aged woman wearing a starched cotton saree and sporting a large red bindi that contrasted with her silver hair bustled out of the kitchen at the end of the hallway. Pausing to turn down the volume on the CD player in front of what appeared to be the puja room, she came to the door.

Charu brought her hands together in a namaste. 'Good morning, mami,' she greeted the lady. 'Sorry to bother you so early. I'm here to see Mr Venkataraman.'

The lady favoured Charu with a pleasant smile and ushered her in. '*Tamizh-a?*' she asked Charu.

'Yes, mami. *Eppadi kandupidichel?*' How did you find out?

The lady laughed. 'You said Venkata-raman, not Venkat-raman,' she pointed out, leading Charu through the hallway into a large living room. At the farther end of the living room was a small study. Mr Venkataraman, at once obvious to Charu as the leading man in one of the recently discovered videos, sat in an old-fashioned wooden armchair, reading the newspaper as though the fate of the world depended on his subsequent analysis of current affairs. He looked up as Mrs Venkataraman led Charu in.

Charu repeated her namaste, then took the seat proffered.

'Coffee?' Mrs Venkataraman asked.

'Yes, please.'

'Lakshmi . . .' Mr Venkataraman began and was rewarded with a mock scowl from his wife. 'Just half tumbler, please?' he pursued his case.

Mrs Venkataraman left the room without a response, but from the smile on Mr Venkataraman's face, it was clear she intended to acquiesce to his request in what was probably a daily domestic exchange.

It made Charu feel all the more disgusted, and thus resolute.

'Yes, young lady? What can I do for you? I am sorry, I don't recognize you . . .'

'Sir, my name is Charulata Srinivasan. Charu . . .'

'Hmm?'

Charu sat forward and said in a soft voice that sounded to her so unlike her own, 'I'm here to talk to you about your stay at Palm Grove resort.'

Mr Venkataraman looked as though Charu had transformed into a ghost.

14

Charu had been woken up that morning, as she was every day these days, by her neighbour's loud TV. She had opened her eyes to find her mother sitting on her bed, looking down at her with a mix of pride and pity.

Shakuntala ran a hand over Charu's head and said, 'My poor child. The things you've had to go through.'

Charu had sat up with a start, wondering if Shakuntala somehow knew about her midnight excursion and the dubious videos, before realizing that her mother was being generally indulgent. To her own surprise, Charu did not enjoy the coddling as she was wont to in the past. Careful not to upset her mother, Charu smiled at her and asked for coffee. Shakuntala went into the kitchen.

Charu had let the smile fade off her face as she freshened up and then headed out of her room. She had picked up the newspaper from outside the front door and thrown it aside with a groan. More murder. More depressing events in the world around her. As if her life was not bad enough that she had to wake up to the fact that she was not the only one. Then, as her mother brought her a freshly brewed mug of coffee, Charu had picked up the newspaper again, out of sheer habit.

Horrible or not, this is how things are.

MURDER AT PALM GROVE

At first, Charu had skimmed through the article, not really caring for the salacious details and speculation that peppered the piece. She tried not to look at the photo of the dead body being wheeled through the hospital, forcing herself to look at the image next to it instead: a nondescript man of about thirty in a dark uniform-like suit, posing proprietarily at the main entrance to Palm Grove resort.

'Careful!' Shakuntala called out as Charu had coughed up a mouthful of coffee. She rushed to her aid, picking up tissues on the way. 'What's the rush? Drink slowly and carefully, no.'

Charu took the tissues, mopping up the small mess around her, and then told Shakuntala, 'I've got coffee on my pyjamas. I'll go change. Actually, I might as well have a shower.' Folding up the newspaper and taking it with her, she went into her room and locked the door.

Alone, Charu had unfurled the newspaper again, studying the photo of the manager, Mahesh, at the entrance to Palm Grove resort. Then she had made her way over to her laptop and—plugging in the hard drive with the videos—began watching them again.

She had seen it in the third video. Pausing the clip, Charu zoomed in on the bedside table where an empty glass had been placed, not on but next to the ubiquitous hotel coaster. There was no doubt. It was the same insignia as the one in the photo of Mahesh. She had then gone through some of the other videos, looking for the coasters that housekeeping left as a matter of practice on bedside tables. Then, to be absolutely certain, Charu had searched for and pulled up the website of Palm Grove resort. The logo was unmistakably the same as the one on the coaster. The videos she had recovered from her brother's locker had been recorded at Palm Grove resort. The manager of the resort had been killed around two weeks ago—the same time that Ravi had also met with his so-called accident. This was beyond mere coincidence.

'Charu . . .' Shakuntala had called out from the other side of the door. 'Do you want to put oil in your hair before taking a bath?'

Charu had not answered, maintaining the illusion that she was already in the shower and could not hear her mother. She went back to the videos and began noting down the names and phone numbers that had been used as filenames for the clips. Then she began an online search, which went easier than she had expected, thanks to middle-aged Indians' predilection of sharing their lives on Facebook. Of the twenty-seven contacts, she had discovered that five had given their location as Mumbai; the others were all over the country and a couple of them overseas.

Finding the exact addresses of the five had proved to be a little less direct, but Charu was—with a bit of ingenuity and some online snooping—able to find details for three of them who were clearly new to social media and not cautious about what they revealed online.

Venkataraman, in Chembur, had been the nearest.

'Coffee.' Mrs Venkataraman walked into the room bearing two steel tumblers of coffee as well as a plate of biscuits. On seeing his wife, Venkataraman hastily rearranged his features in an amiable expression, having gone already from shock to fury in the span of seconds. He waited till she set the refreshments on a small table and left, then turned to Charu.

'Get out,' he hissed through clenched teeth.

'Sir—'

'I said, get out.' Eyes bulging and red, he added, 'Get out, before I call the police.'

Charu felt a confidence she did not know she had inside her come to the fore. She stood up and said, 'All right then, sir. I'll just say goodbye to mami. She'll be in the kitchen, I suppose. By the way, does she know about your . . . *enjoyable* stay at the resort?'

The statement caught Venkataraman unawares. He stared open mouthed at Charu.

Charu made good on the moment to get in her bit. 'I have no interest in your affairs or in disrupting your harmonious life, sir. I just need some information. I—I need your help. I think my brother may have been killed by those involved in this. All I need is for you to tell me what happened and I swear, your secret is safe with me. Please—I just need to know. What happened?'

Venkataraman clenched the arms of his chair tight for what seemed like a long time. Outside, on the CD player, the 'Suprabhatam' had ended, segueing predictably into M.S. Subbulakshmi's trademark 'Vishnu Sahasranamam'.

Charu began mentally reciting along, the learning of years translating into an action that had little meaning for her, all the more so at the moment.

Perhaps it was the prayer or delayed resignation on Venkataraman's part, but he eased his grip on the chair and sunk back into its depths. He glanced at his coffee, clearly longing for the reassurance of the familiar taste.

Charu waited.

At length, Venkataraman said, 'What happened . . . was *blackmail*.'

15

David was no stranger to plodding through his day despite hangovers, even waking up when his daily alarm would ring. But painkiller-and-alcohol-induced hangovers were, he decided as he managed to open his eyes to a blurred-looking world, in another league altogether.

'Fuck!' he swore out loud as he looked at the clock, then repeated, 'Fuck! Fuck! Fuck!' as he saw the multiple missed calls from Charu on his mobile phone. The concern peaked as he saw that the calls were made late at night and turned quickly into fear as he tried to return her call but got no response. Her phone kept ringing.

Jumping out of bed, David made to leave, but then caught a glimpse of himself in the mirror. Cursing again, he took a few minutes to wash up and change, all the while trying Charu on the phone over and over. He kept ringing her as he drove to her apartment, right up till he rang the doorbell.

'David!' Shakuntala said as she opened the door. 'How—how are you? What happened? You're such a careful driver, how did you manage to get into an accident?

Of course, it must have been the other driver's fault. So many drunks on the road at night these days . . .'

The irony of the statement must have struck Shakuntala, for her face fell. David, remembering that Shakuntala still knew nothing about the fact that Ravi's accident had not been an accident at all, immediately changed the topic.

'Is Charu there, Amma?'

'Charu? She left more than two hours ago; told me she was going to see you. Oh my god . . .'

Even as Shakuntala descended into panic, David realized he had made a mistake and had to somehow salvage the situation.

'Two hours ago?' he feigned surprise, then pretended to check his mobile phone. 'Oh! My mistake. She sent me a message asking me to meet her at the bank. Don't know how I missed it. Stupid me! Sorry to make you panic, Amma.'

Shakuntala was both relieved and sceptical. 'At the bank? You—you'll go there now?'

'Yes, I'll head over right away. Of course, she must have gotten half the paperwork done already, but I'll see if she still needs me. Don't worry, this is just me being muddle-headed as usual.'

'Okay. Call me once you meet up with her? Or ask her to call? She just doesn't pick up my calls!'

Promising Shakuntala yet again that Charu was perfectly all right and that he would soon catch up with her and make sure of it, David left the apartment.

At least the midnight calls weren't panic calls, he tried to reassure himself. Whatever that had been about, Charu had been safe at home in the morning. But where had she gone? That too, without informing him.

Why would she inform me? After all that happened yesterday, I should be glad if she doesn't spit in my face.

David waited till he was downstairs before trying to call Anand, to see if he had any news of Charu. But the ex-policeman did not pick up his phone either.

Think!

Having no vehicle at her disposal, Charu's mode of transport had to be a taxi. David walked out of the apartment complex and to the taxi stand about two-hundred metres away.

David's first enquiries with the taxi drivers at the stand were rebuffed, but after a nearby tea-stall owner vouched for him—David and Ravi hung out there often—the taxi drivers told David that a young woman matching his description had taken a taxi to Chembur earlier that morning.

Gritting his teeth for having run out of curses to utter, David walked back to his jeep and starting it up, headed out in the general direction of Chembur.

~

'Stop here,' Anand directed the autorickshaw driver, getting out a good fifty metres away from the commotion on the front lawns of Palm Grove resort. Throngs of reporters and camerapersons jostled around, trying to milk the horror of Mahesh's murder during its short shelf life.

Anand paid the driver off then glanced at his cell phone, frowning at the series of missed calls from David. Making a mental note to call him back once the task at hand was done, Anand set off across the lawns, lugging a briefcase with him for appearances. As he had expected, the few policemen who held back the crowds let him through, assuming him to be a guest. The many reporters gathered seemed to be under the same assumption, but none bothered with him. He was hardly glamorous enough to be approached for a soundbite. Anand cast a look at the policemen, searching for familiar faces, but the uniforms on the ground had their hands full trying to manage curious onlookers while trying to conduct some semblance of an investigation.

In contrast to the buzzing grounds, the lobby of the resort was an oasis of silence, though the air was tense, mournful even. Many staff members were gathered around the front desk, conversing in low tones.

The cluster parted as Anand approached the front desk and a harried-looking receptionist greeted him with false cheer. 'Good morning, sir. How may I help you?'

Anand looked around him nervously as would be expected of a guest checking in under the circumstances. He said, 'I have a reservation. Under the name Dandekar.'

The receptionist gave him a sympathetic glance before typing the name into the system. He seemed almost relieved as he informed Anand, 'I am sorry, sir, there is no reservation under this name. For today, is it?'

'How can that be? I spoke to your manager Mr Mahesh about it more than a month ago. He assured me that all arrangements would be made. He said he would reserve a special room.'

The receptionist traded knowing glances with the staff, all of whom broke into sly smiles. Anand noted that the staff were far from grief-stricken at their colleague's demise. An unspoken exchange seemed to take place among the gathered employees, ending as the receptionist addressed Anand. 'I understand, sir. I am not sure if you are aware. Mahesh is no more . . .'

'What?! Is that why there is such a mela going on outside?' Anand jabbed a thumb in the direction of the madness outside.

'Yes sir. But as you can see, the police have already finished their enquiries in the hotel. We will be glad to arrange the . . . special room for you.'

Anand feigned hesitation, as though torn between the need to avoid any involvement in tangled matters and the desire to go through with plans made long ago and much looked forward to. He said, 'Umm . . . there was one more thing I had discussed with Mahesh. Actually, you see, I have a business meeting but it's tomorrow. But I came today itself because Mahesh . . . Mahesh had said he will . . .'

The receptionist gave a knowing smile, clearly lacking the sense of discretion to not conduct such business at the front desk of a five-star establishment. 'Please don't worry. I can make the same arrangements. Why don't you see the room and then decide?' He gestured to one of the staff, who came forward to take Anand's briefcase.

'Sir, please come with me. I will show you the room and explain everything.'

A reluctant-looking Anand allowed himself to be led out through the lobby to the beachfront on the other side.

The attendant walked him on a stone path along the beach, towards the very edge of the property. He then stepped off the path, making his way across the sand for a few metres towards a cottage that was set back in a cluster of palm trees.

'Cottage number 38,' the attendant declared, opening the door to show a clean, luxurious room befitting Palm Grove's status as a high-end resort.

Anand looked around perfunctorily. 'The room is nice, but . . .'

The attendant gave a knowing nod. 'Sir, this is our special room. It is situated close to the side entrance. Your . . . guest . . . can come and go without being seen by anybody. Privacy guaranteed.' He led Anand back outside and pointed to the small gate set into the ivy-covered wire fence.

The attendant let Anand survey the scene for a few moments and then gently asked, 'Sir, shall I ask the lady to come right away or in the evening? Also, any preference, sir? We can arrange everything to your perfect satisfaction and with 100 per cent discretion. Nothing to worry about. Just relax and enjoy.'

Anand did not reply, pretending to be sufficiently embarrassed at having his 'plans' discussed openly. He went over to the fence and gate and peered out through the gaps. The fence led to a maintenance area that could be accessed circuitously from the main grounds. This area too, he could tell, was fenced off at its far end. He also noticed a lack of CCTV cameras in the region of the gate. Of course, the beach being public property was not completely closed off, but enough signage was placed at the periphery to effectively make it a private space. It was indeed a most discreet set-up. But nothing gave Anand any indication to how it might all be related to Ravi's death—if indeed it was.

Anand allowed himself to be led back to the reception area, where he purposively reclaimed his briefcase from the attendant. The receptionist pushed a registration form in Anand's direction. 'Sir, for cash payments, we keep only paper records; no need to enter into the main system.'

A fresh burst of clamour from outside gave Anand the opportunity he needed to extricate himself. Muttering, 'I'll come back some other time,' he began walking out of the premises before anyone could stop him.

Behind him, the receptionist grumbled audibly. '*Saala* Mahesh! Didn't let us earn with him while he lived. Now he screws us over from the grave too.'

16

Charu smiled at the cluster of schoolgirls who exited the lift as she stepped inside. As the doors closed, she let her smile fade, readying herself for what lay ahead. That she already had an idea of how it would go, she realized, was not making it any easier.

Getting off at the fifth floor, Charu walked down the narrow corridor to flat number 512: a better-than-modest homestead which had recently received a fresh coat of paint. The wall next to the doorway was already streaked blue from a bicycle left outside.

Oh shit. Kids.

Charu pushed away the rising hesitation with a reminder that it did not matter. She rang the doorbell.

A woman, dressed still in a nightie and sporting a kitchen towel over one shoulder, opened the door.

'Namaste. I'd like to meet Mr Singh please. Mr Tejinder Singh,' she clarified, realizing that both father and son probably lived in the same house.

The lady, apparently Tejinder Singh's daughter-in-law, gave Charu an appraising look before saying, 'Come in.'

Charu was a bit thrown off by the show of diffidence but then realized that the woman's ire was not directed at her but at the father-in-law, and for obvious reasons. Mr Singh sat in their living room, playing with his school uniform-clad granddaughter.

'There's someone here to see you, Papa,' the lady told Mr Singh before taking this chance to gather the child and lead her out of the apartment. She called out over her shoulder, 'If she is late for her bus again *na*, Papa, you only will have to take her. She can't keep missing school like this.'

Mr Singh laughed and waved an animated goodbye to his grandchild before turning to Charu with the same amiability.

'*Haan* beta. Please sit down.'

Charu took a seat and then a minute to settle her bag on her lap even as she mentally rehearsed her opening lines. 'Sir, my name is Charulata.'

'Yes, beta?'

'I need to speak to you about your stay at Palm Grove resort.'

~

David looked up and down the quiet lane, unsure of what to do next. He was thirsty and his stomach rumbled, devoid as it was of both breakfast and lunch. Despite that, he had not been able to bring himself to take a break, even for a roadside cup of tea. He had been driving around the

Chembur area for most of the afternoon and had already waited on two street corners for as long as he could without raising an alarm. This was his third stop and already an elderly gentleman had approached him to ask whether he was looking for an address or waiting for someone. The query had been made in suspicion and not in friendliness. Just as David noticed the gentleman walking towards him again and prepared to get back into his jeep, his phone rang.

'Charu! Charu where the hell—are you okay? What happened?'

'I'm fine, David,' Charu's voice came over the line. 'Where are you?'

'I'm in Chembur. Where are *you*? God, I've been so worried . . .'

'Could you pick me up, please? I'm at Dolce Ice Cream Parlour, opposite Maheshwari Housing Society.'

'Yes, I know where it is. Am heading over right now. But what on earth is going on, Charu? What the fuck do you think—'

A click, as Charu hung up.

'Bitch!' David cursed, kicking at the wheel of his vehicle, the action bringing the gentleman to a halt where he was. David took a deep breath then called out, 'Sorry, Uncle.' He got in and started the vehicle, its tires squealing as he gunned the accelerator harder than he had to in his irritation.

David drove as fast as he could and was at the ice cream parlour in less than ten minutes. He saw Charu standing outside, consuming an ice-cream cone with diligence.

As soon as Charu saw him, she finished the rest of her cone in a large mouthful, wiped her lips and hands and—throwing the tissue into a nearby dustbin—got into the car.

'What the fuck, Charu?' David began at once. 'I've been worried sick. Can't you pick up your bloody phone? Look, I know I did something terrible. You have every right to be pissed at me about it, but seriously, this is not done. You're acting like a bloody—'

His tirade came to stop as Charu held the day's newspaper up in front of him.

'Do you know this place?' she asked, calmly.

'What . . . what does this have to do with—'

'Do you know this place, David? Have you been there?'

David floundered, but then answered, 'Yes, I know this place. I've been there. Ravi did a photoshoot there—some interview or the other—a couple of years ago. He called me up and asked me to come over, saying it was a beautiful location. I met him there for a drink after his assignment. We . . . we sat on the beach.'

'Did you go back there after that? Did Ravi?'

'I didn't. And to the best of my knowledge, neither did Ravi.'

Charu sighed. 'All right. I need you to take me to Opera cinema, please.'

Taken aback, David let go of his ire. 'Charu, Opera is . . . I mean, you know what kind of movies they play in places like that, right?'

'Porn? Adult films? Yeah, I know. Can we go?'

David felt torn between shouting at Charu, even telling her to get out of his car, and feeling anxious about what he had just heard. He took a deep breath, reining in his temper. Gently, he said, 'We can go there, Charu. But please, before that, tell me what is going on. Please?'

Charu looked directly at him and said, 'Last night, I found a hard drive in a locker Ravi had rented. The drive has videos taken at Palm Grove resort of various men having sex with women who, I'm guessing, are escorts. I've met two of these men. They were blackmailed using those videos.'

'Do you think Ravi was doing a story on this? Do you think the blackmailers killed him because . . . ?'

'I'll tell you once I find out. Now, can you drive, please? Or should I just take a taxi?'

Mumbling the words that he wanted to use under his breath, David pulled away and began driving south, towards the heart of the city. Charu put the newspaper back in her bag, then turned to look out the window for the entire drive.

~

Anand did not have to search too hard for his intended destination; the loud and surprisingly upbeat sounds of a funeral in progress guided his way. He told the driver of the autorickshaw he was travelling in to stop at the entrance to a lane in a government slum redevelopment colony. Cheap posters informed those who did not know, that the entire community mourned the demise of Mahesh. In front of what Anand supposed was the block containing Mahesh's flat was a cloth canopy, under which the body was presumably been laid out for last rites and the paying of respects before it was conveyed to the crematorium.

Anand made his way down the lane to where the funeral was in progress. He observed a woman and two children sobbing over a form that was shrouded from head to toe. Much as he would have liked to question Mahesh's family, Anand knew that this was not the time or the place to do so. He instead turned his attention to the gathered crowd. His eyes fell on a group of four men who stood some ways back from the proceedings. The four seemed more angry than grief-stricken and were engaged in an animated conversation. As he walked up to them, Anand caught snatches of conversation about 'that bitch Shalini' and the men's intent to 'deal with her'. They fell silent as he approached.

'Who here is looking after Mahesh's affairs?' Anand asked, frowning.

The men were immediately on the defensive. 'Why do you want to know?' one of them asked.

'He owes me money. Lots of money. Whom should I ask about it?'

The men exchanged glances. One of them looked over at the mourning widow, another shook his head at him. Finally, the first man said, 'Shalini. His keep. For a man who was just a hotel manager, even at a five-star hotel, he used to blow up a lot of money on her. Even bought her a flat in one of those private apartment complexes.'

The fourth man, who seemed to be the least antagonized of the lot, resumed the argument. 'How do you know all this? Sure, he may have had another woman, but how can you say he spent all his money on her? He has . . . had a wife and two children, for pity's sake!'

'Because,' the first man replied, 'I once took his wife to that woman's flat at her request. Mahesh's son was running a high fever and the poor lady did not even have money for a doctor. You should have seen the way he treated her then. Threw twenty thousand in her face and told her never to come there again. Poor thing.'

'I knew it!' one of the others chimed. 'I knew he was no good. Even though he made the largest contributions every year during the Ganesh festival and Ambedkar Jayanti celebrations. *Chutiya saala!*'

Anand intervened, 'This . . . Shalini, was it? Do you know where she lives?'

'Why do you want to know?'

'Like I said, Mahesh owed me money.'

The prospect of getting Shalini into trouble seemed to please the men, and they readily parted with Shalini's address.

Anand thanked them and left, but not before dropping two five-hundred-rupee notes into the aluminum vessel that was the community's contribution towards Mahesh's funeral expenses. He cast a last look at the woeful widow and her children.

Murder, he had realized over the years, was far worse on those left living than those it claimed. But the admission still jarred him every single time. Indulging in an Ola cab, Anand headed straight home. He knew there were still some hours left in the day. Perhaps he could do more, but he suddenly felt he had had enough. Old age, he told himself, stretching the excuse long enough to bring himself to switch off his phone for the rest of the ride home.

17

Opera cinema was a ramshackle movie hall, one loose brick away from being knocked down to make way for yet another mall in the middle of the city. The smell of urine and disrepute hit Charu and David as they turned into the large open area in front of the theatre that served as its parking lot. A parking attendant came up immediately, taking a visible step back as he saw Charu sitting in the passenger's seat. David ignored the man as he paid for parking and took the paper token.

Oblivious to the many stares that were now coming her way, Charu got down from the jeep and made her way towards the movie hall, dispelling the chance onlookers were still affording her of being in search of nothing more than cheap parking. The stares grew into silent sniggers and hushed exchanges that she still did not notice. David looked around them, then sighing loudly followed her.

Charu's appearance was met with a leer from the man in the wire-mesh ticket booth.

'Welcome madam, welcome,' he said, running his eyes up and down her body in appraisal before adjusting his crotch. He then glanced at David and said, 'Private seats? I'll give you the most comfortable seats in the theatre. Guaranteed enjoyment.'

Charu ignored the entirety of his remarks. Pulling out her phone, she showed him a photo of Mahesh that she had downloaded from the Palm Grove website. 'Have you seen this man? Has he come here?'

'No.'

'At least take a look!' Charu insisted.

The ticket vendor scratched his two-day stubble as if to think, but it turned out to be for show. He sat forward and said, 'Madam, let me tell you one thing. The men who come here neither want to be seen nor do they see anything but what interests them, most of which happens on the screen.'

Charu did not rise to the bait. 'What about him?' She then held up a photo of Venkataraman that she had pulled off his Facebook page. The ticket seller looked, but did not respond.

'Him?' Charu scrolled through a series of photos on her phone, all downloaded off the Internet.

The man looked at each one, but then shook his head. Resuming his cheeky tone, he said, 'Most of the men who come here are like this only . . . middle-aged or even older family men, like the ones in your photos. They come and go in dozens, hundreds even. Any of these men could have come and gone and I would have never noticed.'

David chipped in. 'Are you the only one on duty at the ticket booth? Is there anyone else who might have noticed these men?'

The employee turned grudgingly to David, as though loath to look at anyone but Charu. 'I am the only one here. Inside, there is a cleaner. He has been working here for over ten years and no longer cares for anything other than the stains on the theatre floor. He doesn't even watch the movies any more.'

A disappointed Charu turned away from the ticketing booth and considered the entrance to the movie hall, wondering whether it was worth going in to investigate further. She decided against it and began to walk away.

'Arre, madam! At least tell me before you go, no . . . which of these men is your father? Or are they all—'

David, who had begun following Charu, spun around with his fists clenched and ready for a fight.

'No, David.' Charu restrained him with a hand on his chest. 'It's not worth it.'

'But Charu—'

'We've got better things to do. Never mind. Let's go.' She pulled on David's arm for emphasis, getting him to fall in next to her.

The ticket seller, however, continued with having his fun. 'Go, hero, go! You don't need to bring her to a movie, she'll show you a good time anyway. See, madam, at least when you asked me about that guy in the first photo I could tell you that he has not been here, because I'd remember if he had. Younger men, like your hero here, don't waste their time watching porn movies when they can be getting real action. Arre, hero! Guaranteed action tonight, huh? Arre! Arre!'

The man shrunk back into what he hoped was the safety of his booth as Charu spun on her heel and began striding back towards him.

'Madam, I—' he began as she came to a resolute stand in front of the booth.

David was right behind her, quite pleased at the prospect of finally having a go at the ticket seller.

But to the surprise of both men, Charu did not bother with hitting the ticket seller or even berating him. She simply held up her phone once more, showing him another photo. 'Have you seen this man? *Isko dekha hai?*'

The stunned ticket seller looked from Charu to the phone and then back at her again. He nodded. 'Monday matinee.'

'What?'

'Every few weeks, he comes for the Monday matinee show. I think he is from another town. He always had a bag with him.'

'He came every week?' David asked.

'Are you deaf or what? I just said he comes every three to four weeks. I assume he is in Mumbai for some work or the other and gets some time pass in.' Back in his element, the ticket seller asked Charu, 'Husband hai kya? Is that why you're hanging out with this hero?'

This time, David launched himself at the man, reaching through the broken counter window to grab him by the collar of his grubby shirt and pulling him forward to slam against the mesh. He let go only when he realized that

Charu was no longer next to him. She was already halfway to their parked vehicle, her entire body oddly stiff.

'Charu,' David called out after her. Then, with a regretful look at the terrified ticket seller, he followed her.

David jogged across the parking lot to reach the jeep at the same time as Charu. He opened the passenger door for her; she got in without looking at him. David then circled around to get into the driver's seat, but did not start up the vehicle, focusing on Charu instead.

'Hey! It's okay! It's okay,' he began to console her without knowing exactly what for. But this was a Charu he had not seen in all these days, tears streaming down her face, biting down on her lip to keep herself from sobbing.

'Charu . . .' David tentatively placed a hand over hers. He realized Charu still had her fingers wrapped tightly around her phone, squeezing it so hard that her knuckles had turned white. Slowly, David pried her fingers open and took the phone from her to look at the photo on its display.

Ravi.

'Charu . . .'

This time she responded, throwing herself forward to break down on David's shoulder. 'Ravi is . . . was . . . a blackmailer, David. My brother was a criminal.'

18

'We don't have to do this now, Charu,' David gently said. They were both sitting in his jeep outside a small villa in one of Mumbai's farthest suburbs. It was just before noon, but to both of them it felt like the day had spilled over from the previous one.

Back in the parking lot at Opera cinema, Charu had finally managed to get a grip on herself and told David the entire story, starting with the locker and its contents and how that had led her to Venkataraman, Singh and Opera cinema.

David had been too stunned to speak, not even a curse or exclamation. After some time, he had started driving and they had headed back in silence, forgoing even goodbyes when David had dropped Charu home. They had both spent sleepless nights in their respective apartments.

In the morning, David had turned up at Charu's doorstep.

Charu had been ready and waiting, as though she had been expecting him. David had said a brief hello to Shakuntala and Charu had mumbled goodbye. They had left the apartment, Charu speaking once they got into the jeep, to give David the address of their destination. And now they were here, in an idyllic residential suburb.

'We don't have to do this now,' David repeated. 'We can come back later. Deal with this with a clear head—' he said.

'Clear head? Will your head ever be clear again, David? Will anything ever be the same again?' Charu asked.

'Look, maybe there's some confusion. I've already called Anand Uncle to tell him what has happened so far. Maybe we should wait for him to investigate further before we come to conclusions about what Ravi may have done. This—this doesn't seem like something he would do. He might not have been involved in it, not in the way you think.'

Charu smiled, mollified and heartbroken at David's trust in his friend. She had held on to that trust too, till it had been completely shattered a day ago. 'I kept telling myself that Ravi must have been investigating the crime or some such thing. But he was in on it. Both Venkataraman and Singh told me that they had dropped the money off at Opera cinema. If Ravi was the one who was there, if he was the one who picked up the pay-off, then . . .' Out of nowhere, she added, 'I'm sorry. I was pissed off with you and I still think it was rightly so . . . but I also overreacted. I don't know what I'd have done, would do now, if you weren't with me, David. I don't know what could be worse than this.'

David nodded, not sure how to react, though on the inside he was relieved that Charu was not angry at him any more. As for what would happen next, he simply had no clue.

Charu made the decision for them both by getting out of the vehicle.

'Are you sure?' David asked. 'Are you feeling up to this?'

Charu shook her head. 'It was hard only the first time. Now, I don't think there's anything more that can shock me. In fact, you didn't even have to come with me.'

'And have your mother go all ninja on me? She'll kill me if anything happens to you, you know?'

Charu managed a weak smile at that, though she did feel a little better for David's messed-up jokes and a whole lot better for having him with her.

She walked up to the villa and let herself into the garden, taking in the overgrown rose bushes, the closed windows and the absolute stillness around the house. Her suspicions were confirmed as she rang the doorbell many times, with no answer. No one was home. To be doubly sure, Charu banged on the door for good measure and called out. Indeed, no one was home.

She breathed out hard at the anticlimax, feeling both relieved and disappointed that it had come to this. She turned and began walking out when she heard someone call out. 'Are you looking for Mrs Mehra? She is in Bangalore, at her daughter's house.'

A matronly lady came out from the cottage next door and approached the common parapet wall between the two houses. 'Are you a friend of her daughter's?' the woman asked, adjusting her chiffon dupatta.

'Hi, ma'am,' Charu replied, playing for time to come up with a cover. 'Actually, I'm here to collect Mr Mehra's annual contribution to our orphanage.' Gaining confidence, Charu made as though she were taking something out of her bag. 'We support many children and destitute elders. Perhaps you would like to—'

'No, thank you,' the lady replied and began moving away.

Charu had to stop herself from smiling at the effectiveness of her ploy. 'Ma'am, any idea when Mr Mehra will be available?'

The question had an unanticipated effect on the neighbour. She came back towards the wall and said in a hushed whisper, 'You don't know?'

'Know what, ma'am?'

'Mr Mehra . . . he passed away about three, four months ago.'

'Oh!' Charu did not have to fake her disappointment, even though a part of her registered the selfishness of her reaction. Pulling herself together, she asked, 'I didn't know he was ill. He seemed quite fine when I last saw him . . .'

In fact, when I last saw him, he was at it like a rabbit with a girl not even half his age . . .

The neighbour moved closer still and cast around in instinctive prelude to sharing gossip. 'It was suicide.'

'What?'

'Yes. Even though the family told everyone it was a heart attack, it was actually suicide. In fact, it was the maid who found Mr Mehra's body, sleeping pills, bottle empty and all. But later, when the police came, Mr Mehra's son-in-law paid them off and had the whole affair hushed up as a heart attack.'

The information collided with a jumble of dates in Charu's head, the things she already knew from her visits to Venkataraman and Singh. Tentatively, she asked, 'Do—do you know what day it was? I mean, the day he died.'

The neighbour was visibly surprised by the question, but indulged Charu with an answer. 'Yes, yes I do. It was Monday. I do *Somvar vrat* for Lord Shiva and there is a puja in my house in the evenings. But that day—I mean, it would not look nice to have puja when there is a death next door, would it? Anyway, why did you want to know?'

Charu realized she had got as much out of the woman as was possible without raising suspicion. 'Oh, no reason,' she replied. 'Just curious, I guess. I also asked because I need some approximate date at least, for our database. Thanks, ma'am. Thanks, you've been very helpful. Are you sure you're not interested in knowing more about our charitable trust?'

The neighbour beat a definitive retreat into her house, leaving Charu standing in the garden.

Charu looked down the road to where David waited in the jeep. She could see the outline of his burly figure as he leaned over the wheel. She knew he was looking at her; she could imagine the frown on his face as he wondered what had transpired.

I don't know what could be worse than this. I don't think there's anything more that can shock me.

Something told her not to be so sure.

19

It was evening by the time Anand arrived at David's flat. Charu, who had been waiting in sullen silence, looked up at him with the last traces of optimism in her eyes.

Anand nodded, dashing her hopes. 'Mehra's death *really* was a suicide,' he said. 'I checked with the policemen at the local station.'

He walked over to a glass partition door that Charu had turned into a makeshift whiteboard to mark up the dates the videos had been filmed on and the events that had followed. He pointed and said, 'For each of the shorter clips, there are longer videos—raw footage. These were originally deleted files, but Charu recovered them, using techniques I'm not sure I understand. Mirroring software, did you say?'

Charu managed a wan smile. 'Yes, sir. The hard drive was created using a mirroring software—basically a software that creates a copy of the original drive, presumably Ravi's laptop—on a new device or memory space. Deleted files that are on the original drive also get copied to the new one. Of course, these files are not easily accessible to the average user. We have twenty-six shorter clips named using a name-mobile number format. Each of these is about three minutes long. The longer, raw footage videos have default date-time names. We get a decent idea of what may have happened by looking at the dates and the length of the videos.

Anand nodded his thanks at her and said, 'If we consider the dates on which each video was created, Mehra's short clip is the most recent one. The original footage was filmed on a Tuesday, the short clip was made on Friday and the following Monday, he was dead. There are no more short clips dated after that. So, it seems logical that when Ravi and Mahesh realized that their blackmailing scheme could lead to someone's death, they must have decided to stop. But what was done was done. Something in this whole mess caught up with them, regardless.'

Anand looked from Charu to David, waiting for one of them to say something, to react to his statement. David remained standing as he was, expressionless. Charu, however, got up and went up to the glass board with purpose.

'So,' she began, as though making a presentation. 'Here's what we have, so far. Mahesh and Ravi were most likely in on this together. They set up a hidden camera in cottage number 38 at Palm Grove resort. Mahesh used to arrange for escorts to visit the guests, targeting near-retirement, middle-class men, specifically those who seemed unused to availing the services of sex workers. The plan was meticulous and very disciplined . . .' Charu trailed off as she saw marks of Ravi's fastidiousness all over the scheme but then cleared her throat and continued.

'No matter which day the video was taped on, the phone call asking for money was always made on a Sunday, possibly to catch the victims with their families. The drop-off was always on a Monday: the victims were told to carry cash in a black duffel bag without any design or logo. They were to buy tickets to whichever movie was running at Opera cinema and enter the 3 p.m. show exactly at 4.10 p.m. They were to proceed straight to the last row on the left, the seats of which were broken and unusable. There, they were to leave the bag under a specific seat in the row in front of them, whether or not anyone was sitting there. Then, when the interval was announced, usually between 4.15 and 4.20, they were to exit the theatre.

'That much, we know for sure because Venkataraman and Singh were both given exactly those instructions. We can decipher what would have happened next, based on what the ticket vendor at Opera told us: Ravi, who would have gone into the theatre at the very beginning of the movie, would at an opportune moment, retrieve the cash bag. I assume he must have carried a similar-looking empty bag into the theatre, which he would then place inside the bag with the money. He would then proceed to watch the entire movie and leave at the end.

'We also know from what Venkataraman and Singh have told us that the amount they had been asked for was ten lakh rupees. It's not a small sum, but also not large enough for the victims to risk the exposure and infamy that could come from either approaching the police or by not paying. In fact, either Ravi or Mahesh, whoever made the phone call to Singh, had used exactly those words: was he willing to gamble his entire life, his respect in society and the futures of his married daughters away, just to find out if they would carry the threat through? Or would he rather just buy "insurance" for a meagre sum of ten lakh? And that,' she finished bitterly, 'is the simple brilliance of their plan. Blackmail without greed.'

David shifted, as though coming out of a trance. He said, 'The numbers they used, both to send the videos as MMS files and to call their victims and each other, must have been burner numbers. We tried the numbers Venkataraman and Singh received calls from. They don't exist.'

Charu nodded and continued, 'Coming to the hard drive itself. Although the videos were created and edited on different dates, they were all copied to the external hard drive on the same day—the day before Ravi died. We can also tell from the metadata that the files were copied from a laptop, the model of which matches the one Ravi had. But the police claim that they did not find his laptop in his car.'

'What about a camera?' Anand asked. 'Ravi and Mahesh had to have used a camera to shoot these videos.'

'As far as I know, the only camera Ravi owned is still at home. It wasn't used to record any of these videos, I've checked. In any case, these would've required a hidden camera; something more sophisticated than your usual equipment. No telling where that is now.'

David ventured, 'Maybe we could try tracking the camera down? Specialized equipment like that, there aren't too many places to buy it from. We use all sorts of video equipment in our line of work. I can check with my contacts . . . ?'

Anand shrugged and moved to sit down on a sofa, directly facing the whiteboard. He fixed Charu with an inquiring gaze. 'The camera was not there in the locker?' he asked, redundantly.

'No,' Charu said.

'And money? Did you find any money in the locker?'

Charu felt a bitter taste in her mouth. 'No. Just the hard drive,' she said, even as she registered with a shock that not only did she not trust Anand, especially for the way he had asked the question, but also the fact that telling a lie had come so easily to her. Slowly, she realized that it was not just Anand. She trusted no one any more. Not even herself. How could she, when the person she had believed in the most had turned out to be a monster? And was she any different? She had caught a glimmer of hope on David's face when Anand had asked about money, but had gone ahead and lied nevertheless. And now it was too late to retract her words, at least in front of Anand. She would just have to tell David later that they did have money to pay off those goons, after all.

In a bid to cover up her confusion and guilt, Charu went on, 'Even though we don't have the camera, the hard drive tells us more than enough. As I said earlier, these guys were very meticulous and disciplined. There are a host of full-length deleted videos that have not been edited. If we look at the timestamps on the files, we see they followed a clear pattern. These guys left a clear gap of four to six weeks between each blackmail demand. Also, they never used videos shot around the same time or of consecutive guests. That is, even if three people may have used the room in a week, only one of them would have been approached for . . . *blackmail*.'

'Charu—' David began as he caught Charu's tone.

Charu held up a hand, stopping him short. She continued in the same determined tone, 'My brother may have been a criminal, a cheap blackmailer. He may have destroyed lives and done horrible things . . . but it wasn't two years of blackmail that got him killed. It was stopping his crime that did. It was trying to do the right thing, even if he had done the wrong thing before. I owe it to Ravi to find his killer. What he was doesn't change what I now need to do.'

In the silence that followed, Anand's wheezy breathing could be heard. Then he said, 'I have confirmation that Ravi's network did a shoot at Palm Grove about two-and-a-half years ago, that is, around six months before the blackmail began. From what you said, David, that was probably the day when he called you over to Palm Grove. That might also have been when he first met Mahesh. But since then, it doesn't seem that anyone at the resort has ever seen Ravi on the premises, nor do they recall Mahesh talking to anyone named Ravi on the phone, which obviously cannot be the case. They must have met somewhere or talked regularly, at least using burner phones. And then, there is also the matter of the money changing hands from Ravi to Mahesh. If we can find out more about that part of things, then we might just get somewhere.'

'So what do we do next?' The question came from David.

Anand considered the options for a few moments and then said, 'Breakthrough as all this information has been, Charu, what you did was both foolish and dangerous. If, by any chance, any of the blackmail victims you spoke to were responsible for Ravi and Mahesh's deaths, they might have even attacked you.'

He held up a restraining hand as Charu began to speak and continued, 'Be that as it may, what's done is done. And it seems we have little other choice, but to continue along the same lines. I'll try to find out what I can about Mahesh and Ravi. Maybe you two can speak to the other gentlemen in the videos, since Charu's nice manners seem to work well on that front? I managed to get most of their addresses through a contact in a mobile company. The two other families who live here in Mumbai are currently away.' He added, his tone morbid, 'Of course, technically, they are all suspects . . .'

Charu nodded. 'I suppose the next thing to do would be to go meet the victims living in other cities, at least the ones within driving distance.

'One of the guys is from Pune, right?' David asked.

'Yes. Two of them, in fact.'

'Fine. We'll drive there tomorrow,' David declared. 'What?' he said, as Charu gave him a telling look. 'There's no way you're going alone, so don't bother arguing.'

Charu sighed in what seemed to be agreement. 'I'm planning to send Amma off to Delhi,' she then said. 'I've convinced her it's a good idea to go visit her sister—my aunt—before we leave for America. It's the only excuse I can think of to keep her out of the way, for a while. This is getting to be a bigger mess than I'd expected. I don't want her involved in any way.'

'Good idea,' Anand said. 'On that note, I'm heading home. You guys have a safe trip to Pune. Call me if there's anything.'

David saw him out and then turned back to Charu, who readied herself to tell him about the money. But David spoke first, 'Don't even begin, Charu. I don't want to hear anything about you going to Pune on your own. Even yesterday morning . . . you could have waited for me, at least told me what you were up to. If anything had happened to you—'

'I know,' Charu replied, attempting a weak smile. 'Amma will kill you if you let anything happen to me. You told me that already.'

David studied her with an inscrutable expression for a few seconds and then said, 'Never mind your mother, Charu. *I* don't want anything happening to you.'

Charu stared at him, opening and closing her mouth as she tried to find something to say in response to the warmth in his statement. Then she said, 'I have to go.'

'I'll drop you home.'

'No . . . I'm not heading home. I—I have to meet someone.'

David did not ask who. Charu was glad for that.

20

Charu felt like it had been the longest day of her life and knew she probably looked it too. For a moment, as she sat in the back of the taxi, she debated calling off her date—such as it was—with Jitesh. Two days ago when she had agreed to it, Jitesh's attentions had seemed suspicious enough to her to merit further investigation. After what she had just been through—from Venkataraman to Singh to the discovery at Opera cinema—she decided that perhaps an ill-timed outing was what she needed after all. A drink, inane conversation and what might be a boring evening, all to overshadow the real problems before her.

She also supposed it might help with the niggling guilt that she had still not told David and Anand about the money. While keeping it from the former had been more about a lack of opportunity, she had wilfully refrained from mentioning it in front of Anand. Why? Did she not trust him? Or was she embarrassed about what Ravi had done? Seriously, was there room for embarrassment any more, after what they all now knew about her brother?

Charu washed her face, reapplied her lipstick and mussed up her dust-and-stress limp hair in the clean, lavender-scented washroom annexed to the restaurant. But even so, she felt it did little to improve her bedraggled appearance.

Apparently, Jitesh was of the same opinion and it showed in his expression as she approached the table he was already seated at. By way of greeting, Charu mumbled her apologies for being late, realizing as she did that she was well on time. Jitesh countered with his own apologies for being early as he stood up to shake her hand. Courtesies exchanged, they both took their respective seats, a not-uncomfortable pause in the air as Charu settled herself in, reached out for the glass of water that a waiter had just poured and finished it in one go. Setting the glass back on the table, she smiled at Jitesh.

'Sorry. Long day. But it's good to be here. This is a lovely restaurant.'

'I suppose you must think me callous to ask you out under such circumstances . . .' Jitesh began.

'As you must me, for having dinner with you under such . . . circumstances . . . as you call them,' Charu said. Chuckling mirthlessly, she added, 'Let's make a deal. I won't think this weird if you won't. I really could do with some general, pointless conversation.'

Jitesh relaxed a little at that, but then said, 'Which brings me to the next thing, Charu. I'm not sure if I'm supposed to talk about Ravi and everything that is happening or if I should avoid that and instead ask questions about your favourite movies and the weather in the US at this time . . .'

Charu smiled, this time genuinely. 'Why not begin by talking about you and see where that goes?'

Jitesh took a gulp of his water and then sat forward, elbows on the table. 'Very well. I'm one of the youngest operations heads of a media channel in India. I'm rich, divorced and, I'm told, not bad looking. So most people assume I'm an asshole. They're probably right.'

'How did you end up in media?' Charu asked.

'I was once an investigative reporter. No major stories though, just enough to keep my career plodding along. In fact, I was one of the few old-timers left at my previous company when things started going down the drain. They put me in charge of things for a while, with a fancy title. Turned out, that was just what my résumé needed and when the company shut shop, I got lucky. I was headhunted by other media firms. Before I knew it, I was . . . someone. I've just spent the years since trying to earn that reputation.'

'No wonder then . . .' Charu said, realizing at the curious look on Jitesh's face that she may have found an opening she did know she had been looking for. Dismissing the warning at the back of her mind that this obsession—and certainly this deviousness—was not healthy, she said, 'Ravi. He really admired you; you were his role model. I guess that's why he was bent upon doing investigative stories.'

Jitesh frowned. 'I'm flattered that he saw me that way. But your brother was not an investigative journalist. He did more of human-interest stories. It went well with his kind and empathetic nature.'

'Oh, I know,' Charu fibbed. 'But he was always going on about how, someday, he would land on an exposé that would set him firmly in the investigative domain. I'm sure he mentioned it to you too; even brought you some stories or leads? I thought he mentioned something about that, on one of our calls . . .'

'No,' Jitesh said, a little too quickly for Charu's liking. 'No, he didn't bring me any stories. Good heavens, I hope he wasn't acting on his own, poking his head into something dangerous? Those things have a way of coming back to hurt your family. Trust me, I know . . . it's one of the reasons I'm divorced.'

Charu could not decide whether Jitesh was cautioning her or redirecting the conversation to his available status. If not for his tone, she might have even thought that Jitesh was giving her a veiled threat. Either way, she realized that pushing the topic was not going to make for any form of productive or even pleasant conversation.

She gave in. 'My bad. Here we are trying not to talk about Ravi and I go bring him into it.'

Jitesh dismissed it with a wave of his hand. 'Tell me about your research,' he said, and that was that.

The rest of the evening would have been pleasant enough, had the conversation on US and Indian politics that had filled it not come of a conscious effort on both their part to avoid any topic that even remotely involved Ravi. By the time Charu got home in a cab, having firmly declined Jitesh's offer to drop her, she was too tired to think and was thankful for it.

Charu stifled a yawn as she paid off the taxi driver and began walking into her apartment building, when a movement caught the corner of her eye. She spun around, sleep and fatigue gone, only to find a torn-off wall poster for some political rally rustling across the road, carried by a light breeze. Charu let out an audible sigh. She was going to age decades in a matter of days at this rate. She glanced around at the empty street in front of the apartment complex. Dark, deserted and quiet, as it should be at that time of the night. Or was it?

Fear coursed through Charu before her mind could assess the situation. She ran into her building, punching the buttons in the lift many times in an ineffective bid to get the doors to close faster. She was ready with the house keys when she reached her floor and sprinted across the corridor and into her house, quickly locking the door behind her.

Charu leaned against the door, catching her breath, wondering now in safety if she had overreacted. Moving quietly, she checked in on Shakuntala, who was fast asleep, her bags packed and ready for her morning flight. Then Charu made her way across to the kitchen window and peered out from behind the edge of the curtain. There was no doubt. The same van that had chased her and David just days ago was now parked on the street farther down from the entry gate into the apartment complex.

Fuck!

This time, though, reason caught up with Charu and she felt the panic recede a little. Of course, the men were still following her and possibly had been following David too, though she could not be sure of it. They wanted their money. Except, as Charu reminded herself, she now had their money. All of it and more. David had mentioned Ravi saying he had needed forty lakh to settle his debts, such as they were, but the bag Charu had recovered from Ravi's locker had held, she now estimated, recalling the number of bundles she had counted, nearly sixty-two to sixty-three lakh. Ravi could have, should have, paid off the goons. In fact, he had told David that he was on his way to do so. And yet, the money was still in the locker, weeks later.

Charu let the curtain fall back into place and turned to stare into the dark room. *Why had Ravi not paid the goons off when he had the money to do it? Was his death actually about the money he owed and not the blackmail?* The latter thought was strangely reassuring, as though there still was hope for justice, for in that case, justice was indeed deserved. *Or was there something else, something worse that Ravi had been up to?*

Charu had never imagined her brother to be the mastermind of a blackmailing scheme, but now that it was a fact beyond dispute, it did not seem a stretch to wonder if there had been more to him and his nefarious deeds.

Once you start to fall, can you stop before hitting rock bottom? Perhaps Ravi had crossed an even further line than she had thought . . .

The notion that there were darker depths to her docile brother filled her with a strange confidence, as though his ability for guile would somehow help her survive.

Charu peered out again, in time to watch as the car's engine started up and it was driven away, without the headlights coming on. Her heart skipped yet another beat as she wondered what they intended to do next, though it seemed that for tonight at least, she was safe. She had the money. She was safe.

21

'Take care of her, David.'

'I will, Amma. Don't worry. Have a safe flight.'

Charu did not react to the exchange, annoying as it was. She gave Shakuntala a tight hug and said, 'Call me once you reach. And give Periamma my love.'

Charu and David waited till Shakuntala disappeared into the airport.

'You want some chai?' David asked, indicating the food stalls in the outer periphery that were just opening for the day.

'We'll have it on the way? Let's get out of the city before traffic gets bad?'

'Good point,' David said, pulling out his key from his pocket. They walked to where he had parked.

Charu got in and strapped on her seat belt as David started the engine. She waited for what she supposed was the inevitable question about her 'date' the previous evening, but even as they hit the Mumbai-Pune Expressway approach road a good half hour later, David did not say a word. Charu was surprised to find herself more disappointed than relieved at that. She thought she did not want David nosing around in her personal affairs, but could not deny that she felt a little let down by his disinterest. She glanced at him. His eyes were on the road, but he seemed relaxed. His face held no expression. Was it natural ease or was he determined to hide what he felt? What did she want him to feel anyway?

David seemed to have felt her looking at him, for he briefly took his eyes off the road and asked her, 'Are you okay? Did you need anything?'

'I'm fine,' Charu shook her head. She took a deep whiff of the clean, crisp air. 'Lovely weather.'

'Yes. In fact, this would be quite the day for a drive to Pune and back . . . of course, not that what we have to do there is have a picnic.'

Charu did not reply and David maintained silence for a few moments before asking her, 'Is this how it's going to be, Charu? That anything and everything we say and do has to be about Ravi, about the blackmail? Look, I'm not saying that we need to pretend as though everything is normal in our lives, but do you think, someday, we could get this behind us?'

Charu said without thinking, 'I don't know, David. Do we have anything else in common?'

'Right,' David said, letting his face tighten. This, Charu knew, was very much an attempt to show no emotion.

Without looking at her, David reached over to fiddle with the knobs on the car's radio, letting Kishore Kumar's 'Mere Sapnon Ki Rani' compete with the sound of the wind rushing by for cinematic effect. As David began humming along under his breath, Charu wanted to tell him this was one of her favourite songs. It felt easier to stay quiet, as though things truly were normal, after all.

The silence between them continued till they reached Pune, David omitting to ask Charu once more whether she wanted tea or not. It was Charu who said, looking at Google Maps on her phone, 'Both addresses are on the other side of town, David. How about we pull into that restaurant over there for a bit? I need to use the loo and could do with a cup of tea too.'

David complied silently.

By the time Charu had used the washroom and made her way to the table, David was waiting with tea and a plate of sandwiches.

Clearly feeling better on a full stomach, David seemed optimistic as they returned to the jeep. 'Where to first?' he asked. 'Banerjee's or Gupta's?'

'Whichever is nearer.'

'Nearer' turned out to be Mr Ashish Gupta's retirement bungalow in one of Pune's better suburbs. Charu sighed at the sameness of it all as she got out of the jeep, waving at David to wait. The serenity, the wholesome respectability of a middle-class life well lived and a retirement well-earned that she had now seen enough of to know that it was but a veil. Life, she bitterly noted, was neither as well-trimmed as the garden hedges she saw, nor as symmetrically laid out as the red-oxide garden tiles she walked on. She rang the bell to house number 178/1 and disappeared inside.

Charu returned in less than fifteen minutes, wearing an expression that was more resignation than frustration.

'Same thing,' she told David as she settled into the jeep. 'Same story, same immaculate planning, same modus operandi. Everything down to the black bag and the matinee show at Opera cinema. Nothing new.'

'Are you sure?' David asked.

'Do you want to go in and ask him for yourself?' Charu snapped, before adding, 'I'm sorry, David. I understand. You're as tired and disappointed as I am. I shouldn't be taking it out on you.'

'It's fine, Charu. We're going to have to learn to give each other some leeway. What we're doing is not an easy thing . . .'

'Still—'

'Never mind. Do you mind entering Banerjee's address on your phone? Or would you rather take a break, maybe even skip this one?'

'No. We've come this far. And it can't get worse. One more round of hearing the same story won't kill me. Perhaps I'll even start getting used to it. Let's go.'

Half an hour later, David parked a few metres away from a name board on a gate that identified the house as belonging to 'The Banerjees'.

'I'm coming with you,' he said, getting out of the jeep and locking it.

Charu did not protest.

The two let themselves through the gate, walked up to the house and rang the doorbell. Some sounds of shuffling later, the door was opened by a gentleman in his early sixties. Charu recognized him from the video as the very Mr Banerjee they had come to see, though his appearance and carriage at the moment invited nothing but respect.

'Namaste,' Charu said, bringing her hands together. David's obvious surprise at her politeness flooded through her as irritation at herself. She took it out on Banerjee.

Dropping her arms to her side, Charu said, with all intent to rattle the man, 'We're here to talk to you about the incident at Palm Grove resort . . . and the events that followed.'

Banerjee looked from Charu to David then back at Charu. 'Come in.' He opened the door. 'I've been waiting for you for the past two weeks.'

22

Charu felt a dull buzzing against her side, as though some inner organ was having a laugh at her and rightly so. She ignored the theatrical thought and the vibrating cell phone in her bag that had brought it on to refocus her attention on Mr Banerjee in front of her.

After his dramatic declaration, the mild-mannered gentleman had not only invited her and David in, but also settled them into chairs at his dining table before disappearing into the kitchen. He returned and was now plying them with fresh lime juice and Pune's famous Shrewsbury biscuits.

Banerjee sat down at the table, directly opposite Charu, and pushed the plate of biscuits towards her. Charu picked one up before she realized what she was doing and how incongruous it felt. She bit into the biscuit nevertheless, trying to find the calm certitude with which she had consumed Mrs Venkataraman's filter coffee and Mr Singh's strong tea. She smiled her thanks at Banerjee as she let the rest of the biscuit crumble against her tongue, then reached out to take a sip of the lime juice.

David watched her all the while, a puzzled expression on his face.

Ignoring him, Charu addressed Banerjee. 'So . . . you know why we are here, sir?'

Banerjee nodded. 'Like I said, I've been expecting you. Ever since I read the news of that fellow's body being discovered . . . Mahesh, his name was, wasn't it? I've known it was but a matter of time before the police traced his murder back to me. I didn't know his name at that time. It was just a hit on whoever came to pick the money up from that room at Palm Grove. I wonder if it would have made a difference if I had. Perhaps not.'

Charu and David exchanged glances, trying hard not to let their astonishment show. 'You put a hit out on Mahesh?' Charu asked.

'Yes,' Banerjee said.

'Sixteen months after you were blackmailed? But why?'

It was Banerjee's turn to look surprised. He sighed and let his expression slide into one of resignation. 'Clearly,' he said, 'you police people have no idea of the whole story. No matter. I have nothing to hide.'

David began to speak, meaning to admit to Banerjee that he and Charu were not the police, but he seemed to think the better of it, saying instead in what sounded like an attempt at an authoritative tone, 'Tell us, then. From the beginning.'

'About sixteen months ago, as you correctly pointed out,' Banerjee began, 'I received an SMS . . . or MMS, I think it's called. Well . . . you know what that video showed.

Soon after, I received a phone call asking me to bring ten lakh in a black bag to Opera cinema in Mumbai. I was to buy a matinee ticket, leave the bag under a row of seats and walk out during the interval. I did exactly as I was told, not because I trusted the man who had called me, but because I had no choice. Months went by and, as the man had said, he did not make more demands. I began to think the whole thing was behind me . . . some more juice, young lady?'

Charu shook her head, smiling at how easy it all seemed to Banerjee. But then, it seemed easier to her too, now. 'Please go on,' she urged him.

Banerjee said, 'Then, about three weeks or so ago, I received a phone call. The man mentioned the Palm Grove video, this time asking for twenty-five lakh rupees. He told me to book cottage number 38 at the resort, check in to the room and leave the money there. I was forced to act. I wasn't too sure how to go about it, but it was easier than expected. I went to a liquor store near the resort and asked who in the area to go to if I had trouble. I figured a liquor store definitely paid protection money to some local goonda or the other. Of course, I didn't expect much sophistication, but I wasn't looking for that. I just needed to buy time . . .'

'What for?' David asked.

Banerjee smiled sadly. 'My wife was in the last stages of cancer with just a few months, perhaps weeks, of life left. All I wanted was for her to die peacefully, believing that her childhood sweetheart, the man she had spent her entire life with, had been a good man, a faithful man.

It would have broken her heart to know . . . what I had done. I didn't care about getting caught in the long run. But I was terrified now that the blackmailer had come back a second time. What was to say he would not come back again and again? Or worse, release the video anyway? For me, paying twenty-five lakh to make the problem go away once and for all was worth the risks involved, as long as my wife was spared the pain either way. She . . . she's dead now. She died ten days ago, much sooner than I had expected. Since then, I have been waiting every day, hoping that the police would come. So, shall we go?'

David cleared his throat, continuing the charade of being the law. 'Not yet. Tell us what happened after you contacted the local don. What did you do?'

Banerjee shrugged, as though it was obvious. 'The goonda told me to go through with the drop-off as I'd been instructed. I supposed that whoever came to pick up the money would be . . . dealt with. The twenty-five lakh I left in the room was to be the payment. The day after I had left the money at Palm Grove, I received a phone call saying "*kaam ho gaya*". The job had been done. I did not care to ask for more details. Then, a couple of days ago, I saw the news about a body being found and that it had been identified as the corpse of the manager of Palm Grove resort. It seemed unlikely that it was a coincidence that someone else at Palm Grove had been killed at around the same time, so I put two and two together to deduce that it was the manager, Mahesh, who had been blackmailing me all along. It . . . it was Mahesh, was it not?'

Charu did not know what to make of Banerjee's obvious concern that the murder had not been misdirected.

Banerjee mistook her consternation for shock. He said, 'Yes, I gave in to a moment of weakness, two years ago. And the first time around, I thought it fair that I paid the price for it. But this time . . . my wife didn't deserve to suffer and I was not going to let her. Even if it meant murder. Everybody has another side to them, madam; an unseen side where we hide our darkest desires, our deepest fears and our deadliest thoughts. If you haven't shown yours, it's not because you're a better person. You've simply had neither the need nor the opportunity. Don't think you can come in here and judge me. Now, are you going to arrest me?'

Charu met the old man's gaze. His calm words triggered something in her, and the confusion she felt took concrete form as anger. She asked coldly, 'And the other man? How did you find him? Did that goonda's goons kill him too or did you get someone else to do it?'

'What other man?' Banerjee asked.

'There was another man,' Charu replied through clenched teeth. 'And that man was my brother. You killed him too, didn't you? You killed Ravi.'

Banerjee looked from her to David, perplexed. He opened his mouth to continue with protests, but then something seemed to click in place. He sat back in his chair, composed. 'You're not the police, are you?' Chuckling softly, he added, 'I admitted to the manager's murder because I did it. I did indeed put out the hit on him and I don't regret for a second that I did. As for your brother . . . I don't know who he is or how he died. But if he was involved in this depraved, despicable matter, then perhaps he got what he deserved, though I paid only for one murder, not two.'

A silence followed, peppered by the sound of an analog clock somewhere in the house. Then there was a grating screech as Charu pushed back her chair and walked out, almost knocking over her empty glass in her haste. David, equally stunned but less agitated, gave Banerjee a long, hard look and then followed Charu out of the house.

David found Charu leaning forward with her hands on the hood of his jeep, her body taut and still. She stirred as he approached her, spinning around to look at the residence. David followed her gaze to see Mr Banerjee standing in his doorway, a look of righteous conviction on his face.

Charu turned away from Banerjee with a disgusted look and punched the frame of the jeep, cursing as the pain of her knuckles striking metal seeped through her anger. David tried to speak, but she burst out first, 'We're fucked. We're back to square one.'

'Hey, come on—'

'Don't you see, David? All this while, we've been working on the idea that both Mahesh's and Ravi's murders were related. Now, we know that Mahesh's murder had nothing to do with Ravi's murder, even though logic suggests that both of them have been killed because of their blackmailing scheme. But if Banerjee didn't put out the hit on Ravi, then who did? And why did that person not kill Mahesh too? It doesn't make sense. Nothing makes sense! Aargh!'

Charu appeared to be set to punch the jeep again, but then thought the better of it, getting into the passenger seat and slamming the door shut.

David walked around and settled himself into the driver's seat, but he did not start the car. 'How can we be sure Banerjee is telling the truth?'

Charu looked into the distance with a frown, considering David's suggestion. Then she shook her head. 'No,' she said, 'Banerjee has no reason to lie. A man who admits to one murder might as well admit to two. But in this case, it is a matter of principle. Banerjee thought he was doing the right thing by protecting his wife. If he had ordered a hit on Ravi, he would surely have admitted it.'

'Then . . .' David let the word hang in the air. He started the vehicle, muttering curses under his breath.

Charu looked at him, her expression mirroring David's frustration. 'I know. The other possibility is that Mahesh gave Ravi up to those guys, and they went after him next. But why did they bother? We won't know. We'll never know, now. I'll just have to make my peace with the fact that my brother did a terrible, terrible thing—and paid the price for it with his life. But what about me? What about Amma? What did we do to deserve all this?'

'Charu—'

'Is anyone in the world who they seem to be, David? Everyone, from these seemingly staid uncles to my very own brother . . . they've all had another side to them, one that I could never have guessed existed.' Scowling, Charu added, 'Maybe Banerjee is right. Maybe there is another side to me too. Maybe I'm just as fucked up as the rest of them.'

'Hey!' David spun in his seat. His hands came off the steering wheel to cup Charu's face. Her eyes widened at his warm touch, but she said nothing. Realizing what he had done, David pulled back, mumbling apologies.

'David . . .' Charu laid a hand on his arm.

David did not look at her. 'Sometimes, Charu, people are not as good as we think them to be. But that doesn't mean they are as bad as we fear. Ravi was my friend. He wasn't a bad person. And neither are you.'

Charu nodded, but said nothing. They stayed that way for a few moments, till the awkward stillness was dispelled by the sound of a muted buzz.

'My phone . . .' David said, shifting to pull it out of the pocket of his jeans. 'Hello?'

Charu moved her hand away. She too took her phone out of her bag and noticed that there were numerous missed calls from Anand. She turned to mention it to David, then realized that he was already speaking to the detective.

'Okay. Okay. That's useful. We're heading back now. We'll tell you all about it in person. It's—it's complicated. That Banerjee guy fessed up to putting out a hit on Mahesh, but swears he had nothing to do with Ravi . . . I know, maybe . . . right? Yes, Charu said the same thing. Anyway, we'll meet you at the flat. I'll call you as soon as we enter the city limits. Okay, Uncle. Thanks. Bye.'

He hung up the call and turned to Charu, who waited, expressionless. She seemed to have neither anticipation nor strength left in her. David wanted nothing more than to hold her close and tell her that someday it would be all right, that this would be behind her . . . behind them both. Even as he looked at her, something flickered in her eyes, as though she was aware of his thoughts. Embarrassed, he turned back to the road in front of him. 'Hope you don't mind if I drive fast? Anand Uncle is waiting for us . . .'

Charu closed her eyes and leaned back into her seat.

Drama queen. David silently mouthed the words and shifted the vehicle into gear.

Eyes still shut, Charu smiled. She reached out to gently squeeze his fingers as they rested on the gearstick, before placing her hand back in her lap.

23

Anand's day had got off to a later and considerably better start than David's and Charu's, but for a minor grouse. He had set out from his house in the retired police officers' colony, his stomach full of a delightful breakfast that begged for a mid-morning nap, making a stop at Naina's house so that she could join him. As Anand had waited for her, Naina's father and two of his other retired policeman friends had called out to him, asking him to join their carrom board game in the small garden fronting the Mathur residence.

'Hot samosas, courtesy Naina's mother,' Mathur had promised.

'I'm busy,' Anand declined. 'I'm in the middle of an investigation.'

'What investigation, sir? You should be enjoying your retirement, as we are. Anyway, there's no use for our kind of investigative skills any more.'

One of the others added, 'We are old-fashioned, it seems. In this world of modern techniques, all we are good for is tailing cheating spouses or doing background checks for matrimonial prospects. Eh, Mathur! You did the right thing, sending Naina into the forensics line. The girl at least has a chance at a decent career.'

Mathur grinned proudly, then said to Anand, 'So, which nice, fair, well-employed boy with "clean habits" are you chasing today? And how is my daughter going to help you with it?'

Anand laughed and took a seat on a plastic stool, making sure not to get too comfortable. Despite the aroma from inside the Mathurs' kitchen, he had to get going soon. He said, 'No, no. This is quite serious: two men are dead and there may be some sort of blackmail involved.'

Mathur pocketed a carrom coin as he nodded his head in approval. 'Not bad, Anand,' he declared. 'Blackmail and murder. But in your old age, take it easy. No running after bad guys and all. In any case,' he tapped on Anand's belly indulgently, 'not that you can manage that sort of thing any more.'

Dubey, the fourth of their company, laughed out loud and piped in, 'And, Anand, don't forget the fundamental rule of a blackmail case: you cannot believe anyone, because everyone has something to hide. Even those who are not murderers are far from saints.'

Anand smiled as a vision of the portly Singh and the other distinguished gentlemen in the Palm Grove videos flashed across his mind. 'Indeed,' he told Dubey, 'there appear to be many saints—just like you and I—involved in this case. Makes me wonder, you know. Do we ever really know the whole truth about anyone?'

Mathur had considered the weighty statement. 'Do we need to?' he asked. 'Don't get too philosophical in your old age, Anand. The best thing about the law is that right and wrong are far too clear for us to have moral compunctions about what we do . . . what we did, rather. If you are going to do police work, then you can't afford not to think like a policeman.'

'Good thing I have your daughter to help me, then,' Anand had said, standing up in preparation to leave, as Naina emerged from the house.

Anand had slapped Mathur on the back and wished his other friends a good day, before he and Naina made their way to the train station. But Mathur's words had stayed with him all the way to their destination: an upper-middle-class apartment complex in a residential suburb not too far from Palm Grove resort. It was here that Mahesh had settled his girlfriend, Shalini.

Shalini, it turned out, had been less surprised by Anand and Naina's arrival and more so by the respectful tone in which Anand asked for her through the few inches that she opened her door for. Peering at them, she narrowed her eyes in momentary suspicion, the concealer she had used to try and hide her sorrowful dark circles creasing as she did.

Anand instinctively said, 'I'm so sorry for your loss. How are you doing, beta?'

In response, Shalini opened the door and invited them both in.

'Please sit,' she pointed towards the Italian faux-leather sofa and disappeared into the kitchen. Naina sat down on the indicated sofa, while Anand settled himself into a plush single-seater armchair and took in the simple but tastefully decorated room. Next to the TV, he noticed, was a framed picture of Shalini and Mahesh on holiday at some beach destination. Anand suspected that it was a far more exotic place than Palm Grove resort.

Shalini reappeared with three cups of tea on a tray. Setting the tray down on a low table, she took a seat on a beanbag, crossing her bare legs. As Anand had expected, she seemed to find some comfort in Naina's presence, asking her, 'How did you know Mahesh?'

Naina replied, 'Sir here is looking into his death. Some . . . friends of Mahesh's . . . believe that little will come of the police investigation. They want to get at the truth.'

Shalini sniggered and looked at Anand. 'That explains your politeness, then. Most people who have come looking for me since Mahesh died rarely bother to use my name. "slut", "bitch" . . . and of course, his wife's favourite: "*chudail*".'

Anand held his palms up in a gesture that indicated he had no interest in judging Shalini. She picked up her tea, indicating that her visitors did the same.

Anand took a sip of the beverage. 'How did you meet Mahesh?' He did not add that he already knew that Shalini had once been a high-priced escort before she and Mahesh had set up together about five or six years ago.

Shalini shrugged. 'Everyone knows the story,' she said. 'I used to work at Palm Grove. Mahesh and I fell in love and he then bought out my . . . contract . . . from the man I was working for.'

'So . . . this business of arranging for escorts . . . Mahesh had been doing it for quite sometime?'

'Since about the time we met. He had joined Palm Grove as manager just some months before I started working there. I don't know how he got into it, but I'm not surprised. These arrangements are very common at all the big hotels here, even the five- and six-star ones.' She added, without Anand having asked, 'Mine is the same old story. Small-town girl comes to Mumbai with dreams of joining the movies. After a couple of years of "doing favours", you realize you're getting poorer, but not younger. But the dream remains and you try to make money to keep living here . . . and you keep trying. Then, like most women, you find yourself a husband—or something like it—and try to settle down. Actually, mine is quite the fairy tale. Most women have it a lot worse. They don't find love or good men like Mahesh.'

Anand gently guided the conversation back to the topic. 'So, you know how Mahesh ran his operations, I suppose? Can you tell me more about it?'

Shalini's innate distrust of people resurfaced. She asked, in a grating tone, 'Eh, I thought you were investigating his murder, Uncle. Why do you want to know about the business? And who is this girl with you?'

'Isn't it obvious? What Mahesh was doing may well have been the reason why he got killed.'

'It's not that easy. Stuff like this is part of a racket. There is protection money, procedure even. Else the business cannot run.'

Naina said, 'And yet, he was killed.'

Shalini sighed. 'I'm not sure what you think Mahesh was doing, but he wasn't running a brothel. In fact, he called it "good customer service". If a guest at a five-star hotel like Palm Grove asks for a pack of cigarettes or a bar of soap, it is expected that the manager would send out for it if it isn't available with them, right? Same logic. Some guests would ask for escorts. Mahesh would arrange for the girls,' Shalini said.

'Of course, he also used to say that some guests would not know how to ask, though it would be clear from their expressions that that was what they wanted. Then, Mahesh would have to broach the matter himself, discreetly ask the guest if someone would be joining them . . . or did they want someone to join them. Maybe it was because of . . . of what I used to do, but he was very, very respectful to the girls. He made sure they weren't harassed, treated them well. He—he was an amazing man . . .'

Anand waited as Shalini hid her sniffles behind a tissue she pulled out from the pocket of her shorts. From the number of times she mentioned Mahesh, from the way she talked about him, theirs had surely been more than a relationship of lust or commercial advantage. Once she put the tissue away, he asked her, 'I'm so sorry to do this, but I have to ask. Do you have any ideas as to why Mahesh was murdered? Did he say or do anything suspicious in the days leading up to his death? Of course, I'm sure the police have asked you this already.'

'The police . . .' Shalini briefly traded in her pain for disgust. 'All the police asked me was whether I was responsible for his death, who had I now trapped that I wanted Mahesh dead. But to answer your question, I think you already know that he was up to something, don't you?'

'Ms Shalini, I—'

'It's okay, Uncle. I'll tell you what I know, but I don't know much. He told me not to ask too many questions. But he was up to something. He suddenly had a lot more money these past couple of years.'

'You don't know where it was coming from?'

'If you mean how he was making the money . . . no, I have no idea. But every couple of months or so, a man would come here. Mahesh would go down to the apartment gate to meet him. He would come back with a bundle of cash, wrapped up in newspapers. Do you think that man killed him?' Shalini asked.

In response, Anand pulled out his phone and showed her a photo of Ravi. 'Was this the man?'

Shalini peered at the phone, but then shook her head. 'I don't know. I never got a good look at him. He came in the evenings and the street lights usually weren't on at that time. I could see their heads over the compound wall, from that window there, but I never saw the man's face clearly. He—he was a little taller than Mahesh. That's all I noticed.'

Anand nodded. Ravi, he noted, would have been a little taller than Mahesh. As would have been a million other men in Mumbai.

As he wondered whether there was anything more to be got out of Shalini, she offered, 'I have the last bundle the man gave him. It's in Mahesh's safe box, inside his cupboard. I haven't spent any of it. It's—it's all the money I have.'

'May I see it?'

Shalini nodded and disappeared inside. She returned with a small metal box that she had already opened with a numeric combination and a sudden reluctance. 'You—you won't need to take the money, will you?' she asked Anand.

'No,' Anand reassured her. 'I just want to see it . . . if you don't mind, that is.'

Shalini set the box down on the table and then stood with her arms crossed, visibly impatient to get it back.

Anand smiled his thanks and looked into the box. It contained, as Shalini had said, a bundle wrapped in a newspaper and held together with neatly cut strips of Sellotape. It also contained a cheap, but hardly used smartphone. Anand took the bundle out and looked it over. The newspaper, he noted, was a common English daily and was dated about a month before Mehra had died by suicide.

'This was the last bundle Mahesh received?' he confirmed.

'Yes,' Shalini said.

Anand then passed the bundle to Naina, who dug through her bag to pull out a small pouch that held a brush and some other equipment. Placing the bundle on the coffee table before, she began dusting it for fingerprints.

'What—what are you—'

'Don't worry, Ms Shalini,' Anand reassured her. 'We are not interested in the money, only in information that can help us find Mahesh's killer.' He then watched as Naina carefully pulled fingerprints from the Sellotape on the bundle.

Naina looked at Shalini. 'Have you ever been arrested?' she asked.

'No,' Shalini indignantly replied.

'What about Mahesh?'

This time, Shalini hesitated before nodding her head to say yes.

'Would you mind letting me take your fingerprints? It will really help us . . .' Naina asked.

Shalini looked to Anand, who smiled reassuringly at her, before sitting down and wiping her hands against her shorts.

'Thank you.' Pulling out an ink pad and a sheet of white paper from her bag, Naina set about taking Shalini's fingerprints.

Once they were done, Shalini held her hand out for the bundle.

Naina handed the money over to Anand, saying, 'I've got two partials off the Sellotape. If I could get the newspaper, I can run it through a chemical cycle at the lab.

'But you said—' Shalini began.

Anand gestured to her to wait a moment and opened the bundle. He glanced at the bundles of notes inside, all well used, calculating the total to be about three lakh. Holding on to the cash, he dipped his other hand into the box.

'Mahesh's phone?' he asked.

'Yes,' Shalini admitted, adding, 'I mean . . . not his usual phone. The only time I saw him use it was when that guy called him.'

'The man who dropped off the money?'

'Yes, he'd call Mahesh on this and then Mahesh would go downstairs to meet him.'

Anand paused long enough to let Shalini's uncertainty grow. She glanced at the money in his hand, then at him and back at the money. Then he said, 'We'd like to take the mobile phone as well, please.' He held the wad of cash out to Shalini as he spoke.

Shalini had grabbed at the money, even as she said, 'All right.'

Anand passed both the phone and the sheet of newspaper to Naina. 'Thank you for the tea,' he said, getting up from his seat. Naina packed her things and followed.

As they headed downstairs, Anand said to Naina, 'Thanks, beta. I had a feeling she would be more amenable to talking in the presence of a woman.'

Naina laughed, 'Oh, I think you would have done fine on your own, Uncle. But always glad to help. In any case, the police file on Mahesh has been closed, so there are no complications for me. I have to ask, though: do you really want me to check for prints on the newspaper? There must be a dozen prints on it, from the paper wallah who delivered it to Mahesh's and this . . . Ravi person, and yours and mine. We'd also need prints to compare the ones on the paper with and—'

'No,' Anand shook his head. 'I was just trying to see how Shalini would react to being fingerprinted, to see if she knew more than she was letting on. But she knows nothing; she's as much as victim of this all as anyone. This is a dead end. We need to think of something else.'

Anand did not add that it also seemed to be the perfect blackmail: no trackbacks, no loose ends. But it was not. Someone had discovered what was going on and killed Mahesh and Ravi for it.

He had waited till he was at the railway station before trying, yet again, to call Charu. His call had gone ignored. He had then tried David's number and finally got through. While he had not anticipated the news of Banerjee's confession, it did not come as a shock to him either.

Saints and sinners. Anand reminded himself of what his friends had said that morning. The difference between the two was a matter of opportunity. If it came to that, he wondered, which one was he?

24

'We're missing something,' Charu said, as she caught sight of Anand, who was sitting on the low parapet flanking the entrance to David's apartment complex.

Anand was about to reply, but reconsidered. There was a look of determination in Charu's eyes that was not to be argued with, at least not right now. He waited till they were well inside David's apartment before saying, 'You're right.' He briefed them on his visit to Shalini's apartment, ending by saying, 'The phone we got is a burner. There are two numbers that calls on it were made to or received from. One is Banerjee's number. The other is another burner: the SIM is registered to a Komal Devi in Chhattisgarh. Presumably, it was the number Ravi used. At least we know we were right about that part of their modus operandi.'

'So where does that leave us?' Charu asked.

'Well, one possibility is—and David said you had mentioned this—that Mahesh could have pointed the goons towards Ravi. It's not unlikely that they roughed him up and asked who else was involved. And that may have led them to Ravi. We know from Banerjee's admission that

Mahesh's death was a day before Ravi's death. Of course,' he added, 'what doesn't make sense is that local goons would have gone to the trouble of staging an accident. Their modus operandi is—as with Mahesh—dumping bodies in the sea or burying them in some godforsaken place.'

Charu pointed out, 'What if Ravi was killed for a different reason?'

'There's no other reason for Ravi to—' David caught himself a little too late, but tried to correct himself nevertheless: 'I mean, sure, he had money problems, but as Anand Uncle said at the very beginning, those guys are more interested in getting the cash than killing the one who owes them. Of course, whatever Ravi did or didn't do, he certainly didn't deserve to be murdered.'

Charu was either too tired or too jaded to take offence. She counted out the points using her fingers. 'One: Ravi and Mahesh blackmail the guests at Palm Grove. Two: when one of the guests, Mehra, commits suicide as a result of their blackmail, they stop. Three: the blackmail start again with a different modus operandi. Banerjee is approached for twenty-five lakh, the drop-off and everything is changed. Four: Banerjee puts out a hit on Mahesh. At around the same time, Ravi is also murdered.'

David tried to make up for his error by saying, 'Maybe it wasn't just Banerjee they reached out to again. Maybe it was also some of the others. Could one of them have put out the hit on Ravi?'

'It's possible,' Anand admitted, adding, 'but it's also unlikely. Two different hits carried out by coincidence at the same time? Though what I'm more curious about right now is: why did they start the blackmail again? And why do it in such a slipshod manner, especially after being so meticulous and careful the first time around?'

Charu sparked to new life as she exclaimed, 'Because the second time around, Ravi was not part of it. Mahesh must have been doing it on his own. Ravi would never go ahead with something after he knew it had forced someone to die by suicide. He would never have agreed. Mahesh must have been acting on his own.'

Anand and David exchanged glances, then favoured Charu with sympathetic looks. Clearly, she was holding on to every bit of hope that Ravi could yet be redeemed. Neither had the heart to argue against it.

Anand gently began, 'Charu, in that case, it's also possible that Mahesh arranged for Ravi to be killed, because Ravi was refusing to go along with this second round of blackmail.' He paused and then deliberately, slowly, added, 'which means Ravi's killer is dead too.'

'Are you saying we stop? That we give up?' Charu turned on Anand with blazing eyes, forgoing her customary 'sir'.

Anand did not reply.

Charu looked away, her face screwed up in an attempt at holding back tears. Then, as it struck her, she turned on Anand again. 'What about the camera? Where's the camera? And why did Ravi need money?' She addressed the last question to David.

David shrugged. 'I don't know, Charu. Maybe Ravi was going to pay Mahesh to not go through with more blackmail. Or maybe Mahesh was blackmailing Ravi himself. I really don't know.'

Charu shook her head. 'We're missing something.' She stalked up to the makeshift whiteboard and started rubbing off the various notes and arrows and dates that had been so meticulously marked up.

'Charu . . .' David called out. When she did not respond, he walked up to her and put his hand on her shoulder, trying to calm her down. 'Charu, listen . . . Charu!' He grabbed her by both shoulders and spun her around to face him. 'You can't do this to yourself, Charu. Ravi is dead and it fucking hurts, but there's nothing more we can do about this! We can't keep living like this! We can't keep doing this to ourselves! I wanted the whole world to know who did this to Ravi. I wanted them to pay for it. I wanted it as much as you do; no, more than you do. But not at the cost of losing you too.'

Charu opened her mouth to retort, but then bit down on her lip instead, trying to not burst into tears again. She gave in to the urge as David pulled her into his arms; she sobbed against his chest, mumbling Ravi's name over and over again as she let the full weight of the past weeks' grief hit her. She screamed noiselessly into the cocoon that was David, vaguely aware that she was soaking his T-shirt with her tears and that he too was crying, silently, his tears flowing down his cheeks to dampen her forehead.

Charu's resolve broke and she wrapped her arms around David, pulling him closer still as though she were afraid she would lose him next or worse, she would be as alone again as she had been just moments ago. David returned the embrace, his silence more consoling than any meaningless reassurances he could have spouted.

At last, her tears were, for the moment, spent. Charu pulled away from David, who let go to quickly wipe his face. Charu pulled out a few tissues from a box on the coffee table and wiped her tears away before blowing her nose into the tissues. Her throat hurt, her eyes burnt and her nose felt stuffy. But she felt a lot better than she had all these days.

Perhaps, she wondered, David was right. Perhaps it was time to let go. She brought herself to look up from the tissues at him and then at Anand.

Anand gave Charu a sad smile. He walked over to place a paternal hand on her head. 'I'm sorry, beta,' he said.

Charu nodded at him, still too wound up to give her thanks.

With a glance of goodbye at David, Anand walked over to the front door and let himself out of the house, closing the door behind him.

Left alone with David, Charu avoided looking at him. She picked up her bag and, mumbling something about it being early enough to take an Ola home, made for the door. She stopped, realizing that her fingers were back in David's grasp. She looked up at him. He looked unusually confused, though a little less upset than he had been earlier.

Squeezing her fingers, he said, 'Go home. We'll talk tomorrow.'

'David . . .'

He pulled her against him for a brief hug, moving back out of the embrace before she could even think to return it.

'Go home, Charu. I don't think we should say or do anything at a moment like this. This is weird . . . really weird.'

The words slipped out of Charu, 'Murder, blackmail, not to mention that my brother—your best friend—is dead. Weird is an understatement. Take care of yourself, David.'

'Goodnight, Charu.'

The sky had turned an inky blue and street lights were starting to flicker on as Charu, puffy-eyed but in control of herself, paid the cab driver. She looked up at her apartment, the darkness pouring out through the window. Shakuntala, she remembered, was in Delhi and Charu would be all alone in the house that night. Surprisingly, Charu felt not in the least afraid at the prospect. She wanted to be alone and could sense that David felt the same way too, having failed to even make his customary offer to drop her. Or perhaps he was being rightfully cautious. In their respective emotional state, they might just have ended up doing things they would later regret, especially if there was to be any chance at . . . Charu caught herself mid-thought, chastising herself at once for letting her mind go there.

She then sighed and resolved to let it wander where it would. Anything to distract herself, anything to not have to think about what now, what next. She trudged her way into the building and, taking the lift to the empty apartment, went straight to bed.

Sleep eluded Charu, and she tossed and turned for an hour. Giving up, she sat up in bed and reached for the book she had picked off David's shelf the other day: *The Adventures of Sherlock Holmes*. A boarding pass was tucked inside the book marking the page where David had paused or, more likely, life—or in this case—death had intruded to make him pause.

Charu imagined David on the flight to Kathmandu, flirting genially with the stewardess or perhaps his neighbour. She thought of how his cheeks would be flushed red from the trek to the Everest base camp, of his long legs stretched out by some campfire as he gazed up at the stars . . . of the firm set of his jaw as he received Jitesh's message that Ravi was dead. She saw him falling to his knees on the snow, his tears hotter against his cheek for the stinging wind, the unbearable weight of the journey back, spent staring mindlessly out of taxi windows in a bid to come to terms with the fact that a life was gone, an existence reduced to memories that would someday fade . . . No, that had been her, her thoughts, her dull pain from the moment she had received that terrible phone call, all the way to now, with her memories of Ravi already written over like some data file, corrupted with details of five-star resorts and middle-aged men, of an endless stream of phone numbers and semi-detached houses with rose bushes in their gardens, rose bushes grown wild as their caretakers died one by one in the dingy confines of the decrepit Opera cinema as her brother watched them, a black duffel bag slung over his shoulder.

'Fuck!' she cursed out loud, then set the book aside and got out of bed.

Deciding that a drink was a more effective antidote to her restlessness, Charu poured the last of her brother's whiskey into a glass and made her way over to the kitchen window. She looked emotionlessly out at the street, noting almost with relief that the red Maruti van was in its customary place down the road. It would not do, she admitted with a mirthless chuckle, for all the drama in her life to cease at once.

Charu resisted the temptation to wave at the men she knew would be watching, thinking it unwise as well as far too movie-like to actually have any effect. She turned away and took a sip of her drink, realizing that with all that had happened during the day, she had yet again forgotten to tell David about the money in Ravi's locker. *Or had she really forgotten?*

Charu slammed her glass down on the counter and reached into her bag nearby, for her phone. David was right, this sort of trustless existence, this dark, endless suspicion would indeed destroy them. She could not go on this way. She had to tell him about the money. She had to set him at ease.

Charu paused, her thumb hovering over the keypad.

What are we missing?

Picking up her glass again, Charu took a long sip before glancing out the window once more at the van and the lurking shadows of the men within.

Charu shook her head, pulled up a number and hit the call button.

25

'Wake up, David.'

David opened his eyes to what he was sure was inside a dream: Charu, her wild hair framed by the morning light, her eyes gleaming, her lips saying his name as he had hoped she someday would.

'Charu . . .' he reached his hand out, assured that at least in his dreams he could draw her close, hold her to him and kiss her and tell her all the things he had wanted to say to her. And now, this dream, that was so real, so, so real . . . that the cheery visage of Anand Uncle smiled down at him.

David was awake in a second and all the more aware of the fact that he was in bed, wearing nothing more than a pair of boxer shorts. He pulled the crumpled bed sheet to cover as much of his near-naked form as he could without making a show of it.

'You forgot to lock your front door,' Charu explained, suppressing a chuckle at his embarrassment. 'I'll go make some tea,' she said, moving out of his bedroom.

David watched her, then favoured the waiting Anand with a pointed look. Then, pragmatism got the better of him. 'What are you both doing here? What time . . . shit, it's just 7 a.m. Is everything okay?'

In response, Anand smiled and said, 'It's better than okay. This girl . . . she's smarter than most people I've met. Now, get up. We have work to do.'

David pointedly remained as he was.

Anand mumbled something about a three-year-old David running around in a worse state of undress before leaving the room.

David let out a long breath and threw himself back against his pillow. He closed his eyes in a bid to let the dream, such as he hoped it was, take him again. Then, with a sigh and curse, he pulled himself out of bed and made his way to the bathroom.

By the time David entered his living room, considerably more clothed than he had been a short while ago, he found Charu and Anand sitting comfortably, sipping tea. He looked from the steaming cup that awaited him on the table to Anand and then Charu.

'Okay, what did I miss?'

Anand replied, 'Not just you, David. We all missed it.' He closed and opened his eyes in a moment of self-recrimination. Then he sullenly admitted again, 'Yes, we all missed it. Anyway, what we need now is some amount of good old-fashioned police work that we haven't as yet put in. Like it or not, we have to go through every minute of video footage that we have, a few times over if need be.'

David jerked his head in what he supposed was a discreet manner at Charu, suggesting to Anand that watching sex videos in her presence might not be in good taste.

Charu noticed. Rolling her eyes, she sat back and said, 'Let's get started. David, would you plug the hard drive and your laptop in and switch on the TV, please?'

Anand crossed his legs in a business-like manner and took a sip of his tea before giving David a pointed look.

Sighing, David did as he was instructed. The first of the videos began to play. David hit the mute button as a woman's well-faked lustful moans blasted on the speakers.

'Leave the volume on. We need to hear everything that might have been said,' Charu immediately said.

In response, David handed Charu the remote. Mumbling something about his tea having gone cold, he went into the kitchen. By the time he came out, a good twenty minutes later, the man he now knew as Mr Singh was having the time of his life on the screen. The clip blipped abruptly into blackness.

Taking advantage of the momentary lull before the next movie began to play, David asked, 'What's the point of this? What are we looking for?'

Anand said, 'We'll know it when we see it. I suspect, though, that it might not be in the edited clips, but better safe than sorry.'

David frowned as yet another raunchy scene filled his screen. 'We're watching the whole thing then?'

'Yes,' Charu said, without taking her eyes off the TV.

David sighed. 'In that case, we'd better take turns watching. Who wants to go first?'

But Charu and Anand were already intent on the scene before them, their eyes oblivious to the act itself, as they scanned every inch of the screen for clues.

'Right,' David said. 'I'll just order some food then.'

'*Chindian* please,' Charu called out. She turned around and flashed him a smile. 'I don't get much of that, back in the US . . .'

David wondered if he were dreaming all over again and if so, could he please not wake up for a while. Then, as another fake moan filled the air, he figured this was not the stuff of his dreams, after all. He retreated to his room and stayed there till he was summoned by the ring of the doorbell.

Charu hit the pause button as David emerged from his bedroom to make his way to the front door, but a glance at the screen told him it was unnecessary. They were finished with the twenty-odd three-minute clips and were now staring at the image of an empty hotel room: one of the unedited videos on the hard disk.

David collected and paid for their brunch, took the packages to the dining counter and began to open them. To his surprise, Anand and Charu left the video on pause and joined him. The three enjoyed a quick and silent meal, Anand and Charu finishing first to clear things away while David wolfed down American chop suey. He swallowed the last of it and got up just as Charu was headed back to the living room, beating her to the remote control.

'Go take a break, Charu,' he said. 'Take a nap. You haven't slept much last night; I can tell from your dark circles.'

Charu hesitated but then, at a nod from Anand, smiled at David and headed for his bedroom.

David settled himself in the seat she had recently vacated. 'You ready for this, Uncle?'

Anand indulgently said, 'One is never ready for this, David. But we do it, that is all.'

Sighing, David pressed the play button. An empty room continued to fill the screen, the occasional flicker of the screen the only sign that time was, indeed, passing. He set the video at a slow fast forward, well aware that the smallest of the unedited videos had a four-hour runtime. He offered, 'Uncle, why don't you take a break as well? There's a guest room . . .'

Anand smiled. 'Why don't you make some more tea?'

26

Charu stretched out on David's unmade bed. The sheets held a roughness that indicated they needed changing, but were far from filthy. She curled up on her side and pulled the light quilt up to her neck. David's smell—his aftershave—filled her nostrils, as it had when he had held her close the previous day. She did not know when she had fallen asleep, but when she jerked upright into sudden wakefulness, Charu realized that many hours had passed, after all. The fading light outside told her that the day was on the edge of evening. Washing her face and retying her hair into a no-fuss ponytail, she joined the others.

'What's been happening?' she asked, looking at the paused video on-screen, of a figure asleep in a hotel room.

'Ah, you're up. Good, we were going to wake you up anyway,' Anand said.

'You found something?'

David replied, 'For the most part, it was an unbearably long advertisement for Viagra. Following which, our leading man goes to sleep. Then, this happens.' He hit the play button as Charu sat down.

On the screen, the middle-aged occupant of the room woke up and began moving about. He disappeared into the washroom, then returned. Heading for the room door, he opened it, retrieved the newspaper and sat down to read it. After a while, the doorbell rang. The man opened the door again and room service brought in his breakfast. He continued to read the newspaper as he ate his breakfast, for what felt like an interminable eternity to the watching Charu. Another ring of the doorbell. Folding away his newspaper, the man attended the door again, opening it halfway. The camera angle, however, was in their favour and Charu could clearly see two men standing outside.

The men handed the occupant of the room a briefcase. He took it and immediately shut the door. He placed the briefcase on the bed, opened it a fraction, then closed it and put it away with his other luggage, which he set about gathering. He opened the door again five minutes later. Room service came in to clear away his breakfast tray, followed at once by one of the other hotel staff. The valet picked up his luggage, except for the briefcase, which the guest held firmly in his hand. That done, he left the room.

David said, 'The video runs for another hour or so before someone opens the door again, from the outside. Whoever it is, knows about the camera and is careful not to appear in the frame at all. The camera then shuts down. Presumably, it was turned off by remote control before the person—I guess it must have been Mahesh—enters the room.'

He rewound the clip a bit and began playing it again, even as Anand instructed, 'Zoom in, will you, like you did last time.'

David used the remote to select and then zoom in on a section of the screen, enlarging the faces of the two men at the door. 'That's Damodar Kumar, the managing director of BCC Labs.'

'Who?' Charu asked, surprise evident in her voice.

Anand said, 'Managing director, my foot. That's just a fancy designation, which means nothing. Damodar Kumar is the right-hand man of Dr Govind Acharya, the CEO of the multi-billion-dollar Acharya Pharma Group, of which BCC is a small subsidiary.'

'The other man looks familiar,' Charu said. 'I'm sure I've seen his face in the papers, though I'm not sure in what context. Is he an upcoming actor or something?'

'He wishes!' David snorted, disdainful. 'But you've seen his face enough times in the page-three section all right. He's a regular party boy: Raghuveer Acharya, Dr Govind Acharya's son. You see what this means, don't you?'

Charu nodded, but then said, 'I think I can guess, but . . .'

Anand said, smiling as he had not since Charu had first met him. 'I called in a favour and asked a local policeman to check Palm Grove's off-the-books register. Our "leading man", as David calls him, is Mr Vaidyanathan. About two months ago, one of Acharya Pharma's new drugs received approval from the Central Drugs Standard Control Organisation [CDSCO] and will soon hit the Indian market. In fact, it was all over the news. Mr Vaidyanathan here used to live in Delhi. He retired from the Ministry of Health some months ago and then moved to Mumbai, according to his Facebook page.' His smile grew even wider as he added, 'See, Charu, this old dog is learning a few new tricks from you.'

'This is it,' Charu said, clenching her hands together to contain the rising mix of excitement and anger. 'This is why Ravi was killed. To keep the fact that Acharya Pharma paid their way to get a drug approved under wraps.'

David let out a breath in a hiss. 'This is way, way bigger than we'd thought. And way more messed up, not to mention dangerous.'

'Dangerous or not, we have to get them.'

'Slow down,' Anand cautioned them both, 'Let's figure out what must have happened. There's no shorter clip for Vaidyanathan, so we can assume that if he was blackmailed, it was only over the phone and that he was not sent a video at all, of either his amorous activities or the pay-off. So he may or may not have known what it was all about, how much the blackmailer knew. That being the case, what would Vaidyanathan have then done?'

Charu said, 'He would've called Damodar . . . or Dr Govind Acharya himself. Maybe even panicked and threatened to back out of their deal. In any case, Govind Acharya would've realized this was not just about a corruption allegation. If permission to market the drug was revoked, I'm sure it would cost them millions of dollars. Not to add, if the video went public, it would be enough to destroy his company and put his son behind bars.'

Anand stuck his lower lip out as he added, 'A mob-style hit like a fake accident. Yes, someone like Govind Acharya or Damodar would have the means to arrange for that. Also, it's a lot more sophisticated than the way Mahesh was murdered, which tallies with what Mr Banerjee from Pune told you—that he put out a hit on Mahesh but not Ravi.'

'So Govind Acharya was the one who had Ravi murdered?' David asked. 'Why only Ravi and not Mahesh?'

'Actually,' Anand said, 'the more important question is, how did he get to Ravi? As in, how did he connect Ravi to the whole matter? Ravi decided to stop the blackmail. It was Mahesh who wanted more, who went on with it. Mahesh not only reached out to Banerjee to blackmail him again but let's assume he decided to go after Vaidyanathan too.' He did not add the obvious: that someone like Govind Acharya would have wasted no time in getting rid of anyone he saw as a threat, so very likely the blackmail call to Vaidyanathan would have been made no more than a day or two before Ravi was killed.

Instead, he asked, 'How did Acharya or his goons connect Ravi to Mahesh or to Palm Grove, when we could not? If not for having found the videos in Ravi's locker in the first place, we would have had no clue about Ravi's involvement . . . assuming Govind Acharya is responsible for Ravi's death, how did he find out that Ravi was connected to the whole affair?'

Charu said, 'I think I can guess what happened next. I think I know what Ravi would have done.'

27

Jitesh, Charu noted, looked a lot less impressive in his workout clothes than he did in a suit. Or, she told herself, perhaps it was the fact that whatever respectability he had enjoyed in her view before had now shrunk to zero. Or maybe, she had, for all that had happened in just ten days, become more difficult to impress.

'This is a pleasant surprise!' he said, ushering her into his luxurious penthouse with a hand on her back. Charu stopped herself from flinching at the unwanted touch, with the reminder that what she was here to do was more important than all that she had done so far, for Ravi.

'I'm so sorry to drop by this way,' Charu said, faking a wide smile. 'But I wanted to catch you before you retired for the night . . .'

'You know you are welcome here any time, Charu,' Jitesh said, leading her into the living room. He guided her to a sofa and then took a seat next to her.

A helper checked on them with trained precision. '*Do juice lao*,' Jitesh instructed him, before turning back to Charu. 'Is everything okay? No problems, I hope?'

Charu shook her head. 'No, no problems at all. Amma and I plan to leave the country in a couple of days, so I just wanted to drop by and thank you for all your help.'

'Wow! That's quite soon,' Jitesh said, struggling to hide the disappointment behind his surprise. 'Er . . . are you sure?' he pressed, then corrected himself. 'Of course, you're sure. Forgive me, it was just that I was very much enjoying getting to know you better . . .'

Charu laughed, 'I'm sure your work involves a lot of travel to the US. We're bound to run into each other often enough. And I don't know how much Amma will take to living there, so for all you know . . .'

'Yes, yes, of course. The world is a small place.' He paused to let the helper serve them both an unappealingly healthy-looking concoction that Charu supposed was the aforementioned 'juice'.

Glass in hand, Jitesh said, 'I don't suppose I could take you out for dinner again, before you leave. Oh, and aunty too, if she'd like to join us . . .'

'Oh no, please don't trouble yourself,' Charu replied.

'No, no, no trouble at all. Anything for you, Charu.'

Charu gave an embarrassed smile. She set her glass on the table before them and turned to Jitesh. 'Actually, there is something you could help me with, please . . .'

'I've said it before and I meant it. I'm here to help you in any manner I can.'

'That's really kind of you, Jitesh. There's actually a small confusion I have and it would mean the world to me if you could help clear it up. So, did you refuse to run

Ravi's story on Acharya Pharma because you didn't think it was sensational enough or were you just too much of a coward? Or maybe, you were waiting to negotiate a deal with Govind Acharya? I'm sure he'd have been willing to do anything, help you in any manner he could, to keep that story from airing.'

Charu saw a few drops of juice slosh over the side of Jitesh's glass and wondered if his hand had trembled. She watched him as he set the rest of his drink down, his nervousness beyond doubt as he ran his tongue over his lips. Rich, confident, successful Jitesh terrified of a young nobody.

It felt so good, she noted, to be the one in control, the one calling the shots. It was so good to not feel confused and helpless. She smiled.

'You know, Jitesh,' Charu continued, 'it really doesn't matter why you didn't run the story back then. What matters is what you're going to do now: are you going to break the story of how your own network's reporter was killed while trying to expose the corruption of a lauded industrialist? Of course, if that's not your kind of story, I do have other networks on standby. They'd be happy to run an exposé of a massive conspiracy that may even involve a leading network colluding with the pharma industry to hide a major crime— going so far as to ignore the death of its own reporter in mysterious circumstances. Wow! That would be even bigger news than cut-and-dried corruption, wouldn't it?'

It took Jitesh a few moments to react. 'Get out,' he hissed, jumping to his feet.

Charu sighed and prepared to get up. But Jitesh was clearly reconsidering his reaction.

He said, 'I'm sorry, Charu. I overreacted. But what did you expect? I have no clue what you're talking about. You come in here and say these horrible things—'

'Cut the crap, Jitesh,' Charu interrupted his tirade. 'Tell me what exactly happened and I'll give you the chance to break this story. That would do a lot for the network's TRPs, wouldn't it? Otherwise, you can see yourself on the news as part of it. Remember that cheque you gave me? With your signature on it? How kind of you to help your reporter's family, when even the insurance company and your corporate finance guys were not willing to authorize compensation. Hush money, perhaps? Oh, I don't have to say anything. The other channels will be happy to say it for me.'

Jitesh's eyes widened as he saw the position he was now in. 'You bitch. You bloody bitch. You think you can coerce me into doing this? Well, I'll tell you exactly what I told that fool brother of yours: I can't break a story like this without corroboration. I would expose the channel and myself to one hell of a lawsuit if I did. Get me more evidence, get me something to back up those video clips, to prove that it was a pay-off for the drug approval and not some pharmaceutical samples or random files and papers or any of those things they will claim were in that suitcase. Get me that, and I'll break the story. Trust me, your threats scare me less than what I'd have to face, otherwise.'

Charu chuckled, 'So Ravi did come to you the day he died. And? After he left? Who did you call, Govind Acharya or Damodar?'

'I didn't call anyone!' Jitesh looked genuinely astonished at the suggestion. He sat down again and pleaded in earnest, 'Yes, I gave Ravi the brush off on this for professional reasons. He wanted to be an investigative reporter, but he lacked common sense! I told him to come back with proof, I really did! I didn't sell him out and I know nothing about his death, Charu, though I suppose it was inevitable once he went after a powerful man like Acharya, and . . .'

'You did get him killed, Jitesh. He was a reporter. If you had aired his story in time, it would have stopped them from coming after him. How do you think another channel is going to play that part of it up? No freedom of press? No integrity left in the business? I think you might want to reconsider what you said earlier.'

'For what?' Jitesh sneered. 'You're not a reporter. You have zero cred in this business. No network will listen to you, especially if they realize I've already rejected this story . . .'

'They will listen to David. Oh, you forgot, didn't you? He's with the press too. Now that I think of it, that makes for one hell of an angle—the brave reporter who was bent upon uncovering what happened to his friend, despite the fact that the very institution of the free press let them down. So you see, I think my . . . threats . . . as you call them, should scare you as much as what might happen, otherwise. Having said . . .' she held up a preemptive hand as Jitesh made to speak, 'I will get you your corroboration, so you can run this piece. And David will be the one reporting on it. But you're going to have to work a little for it too. Unless, of course, you're still worried about lawsuits?'

Jitesh stared at Charu, his chest heaving with anger. At length, as the calculation of the risk involved and, no doubt, the considerable benefits that could arise from the situation fell into place, he calmed down a little.

He said, in a last attempt to express his disgust, 'This is blackmail, you know. Sheer blackmail.'

Charu smiled at the irony of it all. 'I suppose, yes, it is blackmail. Now, here's what you're going to do . . .'

28

Charu was grateful for the darkness, not just because it cloaked the transmission relay van that was parked farther down the street, but also because the moment lacked the cynical cheerfulness of her similar visits to the gentlemen of repute that her brother had blackmailed. No bright red-brick cottages fringed by rose bushes, no pervasive smell of filter coffee mingled with incense, no laughing grandchildren or the chants of the *Hanuman Chalisa*. No pretence, not for them, not for her.

She resisted the temptation to adjust the hidden microphone she was wearing under her kurta: fidgeting was often the biggest giveaway, Jitesh had told her. He had come around much faster than expected after their meeting two hours ago, swinging into action to get the equipment organized and putting the studio on standby for transmission from outside. He had also seemed quite delighted to see David, and had shown none of the animosity one might have expected under the circumstances, going so far as to congratulate him on his Everest feature and suggesting that rumour had it that it was lined up for an award or two. In fact, Charu suspected that before dawn broke, Jitesh might even offer David a job back at XTV.

David, on the other hand, had been far too solemn for a man about to break a scoop. Of course, Charu reasoned, she was going to be the one inside the room, the one actually conducting the sting, so to say. Even so, the byline was David's and it was an opportunity that any reporter would have given an arm and a leg for.

It was Anand who pointed out as much, as he, David and Charu had driven to Andheri, where Vaidyanathan lived.

To that David had replied, 'I've given more than an arm and a leg, Uncle. I've already lost my best friend. This isn't work, it's personal.'

Charu had not commented on that, unwilling as she was to let her emotions resurface and corrupt her focus.

Reclaiming her chain of thought, she rang the doorbell. It was a little late in the day to call on someone, though Mumbai, as a city, did not sleep early. Indeed, the door opened to the chimes of the opening song to a popular Tamil soap opera, one that Shakuntala followed with greater interest than she did the lives of those around her.

The thought of her mother made Charu hesitate for an instant. There would be much to say to her, much to explain and convince . . . and hide from her.

'Yes?' the gentleman who had opened the door brought her back to the moment. Vaidyanathan, Charu recognized.

Folding her hands in a namaste, Charu introduced herself, sliding into the routine, such as it had become, of asking if she might come in and have a brief word.

Vaidyanathan led Charu into the dining room, even as a woman's voice floated out from the living room asking who it was this late at night.

'A young lady,' Vaidyanathan replied. 'She is here to see me about something.' He then turned in a wordless query to Charu, asking what the 'something' in question was.

Charu lowered her voice and replied, 'I need to speak to you about the events at Palm Grove, sir.'

Vaidyanathan's eyes widened in what was undeniably amusement—a reaction that took Charu unawares as much his steps—as he continued to lead the way to the dining room, where he gestured her to take a seat at the glass-topped table before occupying one himself.

'So,' he began, 'here I was, thinking that you are a nice, decent girl from a respectable family. But you're a fraud too, aren't you? And, clearly, you and your fellow criminals still haven't learnt your lesson, not even after what happened to your . . . accomplice. Those are dangerous men, my dear child. I'd hate to think what they'd do to a girl . . . maybe something worse than death.'

Charu almost asked him how he knew what the men had done and who they were, but then realized that it would be far too direct and, therefore, ineffective. The sole reason why Vaidyanathan was being so forthcoming was that he thought himself in a position of power; he was showing off. She would have to pander to that sentiment, play him along.

'I can be quite dangerous, too, Mr Vaidyanathan,' she said. You do realize that what I have—the video of what happened in that hotel room—would be worth a lot to any TV channel in the country.'

Vaidyanathan gave a disparaging snort. 'Govind Acharya can buy all the media channels in the country at breakfast, every politician there is at lunch and the judiciary by dinner.'

'You seem very confident. So much so that you're not even bothering to deny anything.'

'I'm saving us both time. If I deny it, you'll pull a phone or video camera out of your bag and show me the video. I'll have to then say that it is not me you see on screen. Else I'll have to make up some other story for it. But once you leave here or even before you do, I'll be making a phone call. And we both know what happens to you after that. As for me, even if you do go public with your allegations, I will have the best of lawyers and years of trial before I get acquitted . . . and I *will* get acquitted. You see, I may not be an important person, but—'

'Govind Acharya is?'

Vaidyanathan smiled and raised his palms in a there-you-go gesture.

Charu stuck her lower lip out as though considering the statement. Then she reached behind her, switching off the small recording device that was clipped to the back of her jeans. She unclipped the device and pulled it out, drawing the thin wire running down the front of her kurta out too. She held it up for Vaidyanathan to see.

'You—'

Charu held up a hand indicating he wait. It was not necessary, but the man's smugness had made her decide on her next move. Taking out her mobile phone from her bag, she played a brief clip of Vaidyanathan in Palm Grove—not, as he might have expected, of him receiving a pay-off from Raghuveer Acharya, but one of his amorous exploits. Vaidyanathan flinched, a new horror in his eyes, one not of mortal but moral terror.

Vaidyanathan gruffly demanded. 'What do you want?'

'We've been live, on air, all this time. Your confession of moments ago is already on every TV screen in the country right now. If you don't believe me, go ask mami to change the channel. I'm sure that as I speak, more media vans and reporters are rushing to your house. If you want to avoid the drama, the flashing cameras and hurled accusations, come with me right now. The police are waiting outside. Surrender and let them take you into protective custody. You can give evidence against Dr Acharya. The XTV network will back you and say that you are an honest government official who had, in fact, been helping with the exposé.'

'Or else?'

Charu stood up, packing the small microphone and battery pack away into her bag in preparation to leave. 'Or else, you can wait. Like I said, the circus will get here soon, and they would love to feature the video clip of your *romance* in their broadcasts. Do think of what that might do to your family? Your daughter is pregnant, is she not? Or maybe Govind Acharya's men will get here sooner. Of course, I'm not sure what instructions they might come with. I mean, now that you are a liability . . .'

She let the implications hang in the air between them, diffusing through to Vaidyanathan. She then gently offered, 'Perhaps you'd like to explain things as best as you can to mami. I suggest you say you did this as a matter of conscience . . . Though I suspect that sort of posturing is not new to you in the least.'

Vaidyanathan grit his teeth as though mashing away the words of rage he wanted to speak. He settled for saying, 'You talk too much. It'll get you into trouble.'

Charu shrugged dismissively, letting the older man have his moment of superiority as though it made no difference to her. She then walked out and positioned herself at the doorway to the living room, making it clear that while Vaidyanathan could have some privacy with his wife, Charu was not letting him out of her sight.

At length, leaving behind a distraught and sniffling Mrs Vaidyanathan in the care of their live-in helper, Vaidyanathan stepped out of the living room. He and Charu walked to the front door, which he then opened.

The night air was crisp and quiet, with little noise but for the chirping of crickets and the muted drone of dialogues on TV. Yet, there was no denying the presence of a police jeep just outside the gate, a young woman of the rank of assistant commissioner and two male constables standing alongside. Behind them, Charu could see David still speaking into a camera that was live. Anand and Jitesh stood to one side, their heads now turning from David's reporting to Vaidyanathan and Charu.

Jitesh gave Charu a questioning, almost imploring look. She shook her head. Both she and David had been adamant that her identity would be that of an unnamed 'junior reporter' and that she would not appear on air or in press. David had insisted on it for her safety. Charu had agreed, more for reasons of not wanting anything more to do with this whole affair beyond that night. And it was almost done.

The beam of headlights farther down the street signalled the arrival of the first of the rest of the media, just as Vaidyanathan boarded the police jeep. Charu pulled out the microphone kit from her bag and thrust the set into Jitesh's hands before beginning to walk down the street and away from the scene. Anand glanced meaningfully at David and fell in beside Charu. Together, they made their way to a parallel street, where Anand had parked the car he had borrowed from his daughter-in-law for the night.

Getting into the car, Charu sat back in the passenger's seat, expecting to be overtaken by a burst of many emotions. But she felt empty, unaffected even.

Anand began driving, taking them farther away from the fracas and to a main street where a few eateries and a local grocery store remained open, despite the late hour. Parking the car by the side of the road, he sat with her in quiet companionship, as though it were completely normal for Charu to feel as she did.

After some time, Charu stirred, taking an envelope out of her handbag and passing it to Anand.

Anand took the envelope and partly slid out the cheque inside it, his eyebrows rising at the figure written on it.

'Charu—Charu, this is way too much. I mean—'

'I—I'm just trying to set right my brother's wrongs in whatever small ways I can, sir. Maybe . . . Mahesh's wife and kids? I don't know, I will leave it to your discretion.'

Anand nodded. 'I'll do what I can, Charu,' he assured her, pocketing the envelope. He then added, 'I still can't believe how you figured the whole thing out. And I'm even more impressed that you managed to get Jitesh to cooperate, not to mention you got Vaidyanathan to rant on record.'

Charu laughed, though without mirth. She said, 'Barely two weeks ago, I thought people generally were honest. Maybe that's why, but I found it very difficult to distinguish the truth from lies. Now, I've slowly come to the realization that everybody has another side to them. The truth is just a tiny detail hidden by a web of pretence. Rather than believing that people are what they seem to be, the world is a whole lot simpler if you begin with the assumption that everything is a sham. Then, if there is anything left at the end of that, it must be the truth, no matter how unbelievable or painful it is.'

She smiled at Anand, this time with genuine warmth. 'You must think I'm such a cynic, no?'

Anand said, 'I think you'd have made a great detective. But then, you'd have also hated the world around you for the terrible mess that it is. So perhaps it's better that you aren't in this line of work. You still have a chance . . .' He paused as he caught sight of David, done for the moment with cameras and the limelight, walking towards them. Turning to Charu with true affection in his eyes, Anand added, 'Take care, beta.'

Charu exchanged a brief but meaningful glance with Anand. 'I will, sir,' she said, making to get out of the car. 'I will, *Uncle*. Thank you for everything. Goodnight.'

'Goodbye, Charu.'

David gave Charu a quizzical look as Anand drove off, waving genially at them both. 'Either he's in a hurry or he's even cooler than I thought he was,' David joked. 'I suppose, then, that I get to drop you home.'

Charu looked up at David, at the mix of tiredness and relief in his eyes. 'Are you all right?' she asked.

'Yes. Yes, it's always weird for a few moments after you come off camera—not that I've been on camera much or broken big stories like this one. But I've heard from others too, that it's a strange feeling, kind of like a split reality. Of course, this story was as much my lived reality as any I've done. Anyway . . .' he let out a deep breath and glanced over his shoulder. 'I'm just glad that Jitesh was more than happy to face the other reporters. I mean, he practically got me out of there as soon as he could. Not that I mind. I just report stories, I don't like being in them. Sorry, I'm blabbering. I guess I'm still a little edgy. I wouldn't mind going back home—to either of our places, I mean, and just knock back a stiff drink before catching some sleep.'

'Okay.'

David apparently thought Charu sounded disappointed because he clarified, 'There's much I'd like to talk to you about, Charu—your future, your plans and mine—and I want to do it with a clear head. I mean—'

Charu smiled. 'It's fine. I understand. Some conversations should begin with a clean slate. Speaking of which, there is one last thing we need to do, before we can head home . . .' She pulled the key to Ravi's locker out of her bag and held it up.

David took a long, deep breath then let it out just as slowly. 'All right.'

29

'Here?' David looked askance at the decrepit entrance to the locker facility

'Yes,' Charu affirmed. 'Let's just finish this and get on with our lives.'

The two of them walked into the facility, following the same routine as Charu had before. The uninterested clerk saw them to the stacks and left them alone.

David whistled as he cast around at their surroundings. 'Not what I expected,' he said.

'I felt the same way too,' Charu said, opening Ravi's locker and drawing out the black bag that had been left inside. She placed the bag on the ground between them and opened the zipper to briefly reveal its contents before drawing it closed, her hand still resting on the bag in a disbelieving way.

David placed his hand over Charu's. 'Thank you. I mean, you don't have to do this.'

'How can I not do this? It's Ravi's debt, after all . . .'

'Yes, but . . . it's my problem . . . or maybe not . . . I guess none of us are safe till this chapter is closed. Come on, let's get out of here. We'll probably find those guys hovering around your apartment or mine.'

'Hmm . . .' Charu took one last look at the stacks of lockers, an inexplicable sense of loss filling her as she realized that here was where it had begun: the realization that no one, not Ravi, not lauded men like Acharya or even someone like her, truly was what they seemed. Here was where she had first lost the hope that she would prove her brother innocent, that some sense of justice and punishment would make up for his death. Taking a deep breath of the metal and air-conditioned air, Charu reminded herself that there was still room for the latter.

She remained quiet for a while on the drive back towards her apartment, before realizing that David was lost in brooding thoughts of his own.

Surprised by that, Charu asked him, 'What's on your mind, David?'

David shrugged, as though it were nothing, but then admitted, 'You know how this country works, Charu. Men like Govind Acharya . . . they get away, quite literally, with murder. How long before he buys or influences his way out of this situation?'

Charu replied, 'I doubt he can do that. Or at least, do it with impunity. I think he might have more cases than he bargained for on his hand. Assault on the freedom of the press still makes for sensational headlines in this country. There will be enough of a media shitstorm to keep Acharya behind bars for a while, especially if the charges add up.'

'What do you mean?' David asked.

'You'll see . . .' Charu said, with a smile. She added, as she saw the red van quietly move forward from where it had been parked in a lightless construction site to block the road, 'You'll see very soon.'

'What the fuck!' David swore, then calmed down as he remembered the money in the back seat of the jeep. 'Let's get this over and done with, once and for all.'

He got out of the vehicle and went forward to meet the men who had emerged from the van. 'I have the money,' he said, raising both hands in the air in a conciliatory gesture. 'I have it all.'

In response, one of the goons punched David on his face. The other joined in, lashing out with a kick that caught David right in the ribs.

David doubled over in pain; he felt his mouth fill with blood from what he hoped was just a cut lip. 'FUCK! Stop it! I said I have the money!'

This time, the words seemed to have an impact on the goons, as they ceased with their punches. Or was it something else? David turned as he was, still doubled over and clutching at his stomach, to see that Charu had also got out of the jeep and was walking towards them, the bag in her hand.

David forced himself upright and turned back the goons. 'I told you I have the money. Fuckers! Now take it and get the hell out of my life.' A moment of sheer and utter panic flashed through him as he saw the goons look at Charu. 'Leave her out of this,' he said. 'Take what you came for and go.' Hobbling back a few steps to place himself closer to Charu he told her, 'Give them the bag, Charu. Throw it. Throw it and let's get out of here.'

His panic turned into shock beyond measure as Charu stood calmly as she was. Her grip on the bag did not slacken. She did not even flinch as one of the goons came ahead to grab David by the collar, then yanked him forward and laid a second punch to his face.

'Charu—' David hissed through bloodied teeth, at a total loss for words. 'Charu . . . how . . . why?'

Charu said, 'Why are you so surprised, David? Didn't you know, any reporter who wants to break the story on Acharya Pharma has a way of getting badly, very badly, hurt.'

PART 2

'It's a saying they have, that a man has a false heart in his mouth for the world to see, another in his breast to show to his special friends and his family, and the real one, the true one, the secret one, which is never known to anyone except to himself alone, hidden only God knows where.'

—James Clavell, *Shōgun*

Two years earlier

David parked his jeep and checked twice to see if he had locked it. Evenings such as these, he knew, tended to run long and it might be a while before he was in any shape to drive out of there. He looked around him. Even by five-star standards, Palm Grove was an impressive resort indeed. The low-rise building was old but well-maintained, giving it a quaint look. Many cottages dotted the beachfront and clumps of trees and bushes filled the spaces that were not occupied by sprawling lawns. *A beachfront property so close to the city?* It was a find indeed. Surprising then, David noted, that it was not one of the most happening places in and around Mumbai and not surprising at all that studios and media houses found it a delightful place to shoot at.

Pulling out his phone, David sent a message. *I'm here. Where are you?*

The reply from Ravi was instant. *Beach.*

Simple as the instruction was, David hesitated, unsure as to how to proceed through the property and to the beach he knew was on the other side. As though aware of his confusion, his phone rang.

'Hello—'

'Walk straight across the big lawn next to the parking lot. You'll see a covered pavilion to your left. Cut through the bushes there—there's a small service path—and you'll hit the beach. I'm sitting right by the sea. Come fast, fucker, the beer is getting warm.'

Grinning to himself, David hung up and followed the directions he had been given. It was a good five-minute walk, even at his quick pace, but he soon found himself on the edge of the sand. A familiar figure sat at the far end of the strip, another man next to him.

David smiled again at the sight, at the sense of familial comfort it always brought him to see Ravi—polite and proper, *seedha-sadha* as they said in Hindi—let himself loose. It was a side that very few got to see of the otherwise staid and simple man. David was one of those chosen few. It was a secret he carried with pride, as a sign of a friendship that made up for the family he did not have.

'Stop staring at me, chutiya!' Ravi's voice came at him.

'Shall I tell Amma what you just said? Chutiya? Where did you learn such words from, Ravi?' David bantered as he slipped off his shoes and walked barefoot across the sand towards the two men. 'Hi,' he said, non-committal to the other man.

By way of introduction, Ravi said to this man, 'See, Mahesh, what did I tell you? It's because of this guy that everyone thinks I'm a momma's boy. Look at him, trying to scare me like a school kid by threatening to tell on me to my mother. Eh, *thevadiya payale*, you think I'm scared of my mother or what?'

Giving the drunk Ravi an affectionate pat on the back, David held out his hand to Mahesh. 'Hi, I'm David.'

'Hi. Nice to meet you. Come, join us, please. I've been hearing a lot about you.' Mahesh drew a beer from an ice-filled bucket and opened it before holding it out to David. 'Start with this. We'll move to other stuff once the evening cools down a little. What would you like to eat? We can get anything.'

'I'm good, thanks.' David settled himself down on the sand and took a swig of his beer. The place was, as Ravi had promised when he had called him an hour or so ago, amazingly picturesque. The last streaks of red on the western horizon were fading away as well-placed lights came on in the property, living up to the postcard-perfect image on the hoarding at the gate of the resort. It was indeed an exclusive place, particularly for the solitude it offered despite being so close to one of the most crowded cities on the planet.

'Off season?' David asked.

'No,' Mahesh replied. 'It's pretty much as crowded as it gets.' He added, by way of explanation, 'I'm the manager here. So, I meant it when I said we can get anything you want. Speaking of which . . .'

David followed Mahesh's gaze to see one of the resort waiters walking towards them, holding a candle-laden cake on a tray. He turned to look at Ravi, who was watching him with a proud, content smile.

'You thought I'd forgotten, did you? Happy Birthday, asshole!' He scrambled over the sand to throw his arms around David in a hug. 'Surprise!'

The waiter set the tray down on a small folding stool he had been carrying and lit the candles.

'Blow them out quickly, before the wind puts them out!' Ravi instructed David. He began singing 'Happy Birthday to You' in a raucous voice as David complied, then cut the cake.

David let the moment catch up with him and, on impulse, picked up a slice of the cake and smeared it all over Ravi's face. Swearing affectionately, Ravi returned the favour. Laughing at the scene, Mahesh joined in, shaking a bottle of beer to make it fizz up and all over the two friends.

At last, the three settled down enough to make short work of the cake and a sumptuous dinner, before laying back on the sand. The plates and empty beer bottles were cleared away and a bottle of single malt—Ravi's drink of choice—passed hands as the three of them took turns at chugging down shots directly from the bottle.

David broke the silence. 'Seriously, that was one of the best birthday celebrations ever. Thank you, Ravi. And thank you, Mahesh, for arranging everything.'

Ravi said, 'I met Mahesh when I came here on a shoot some weeks ago. We got along like a house on fire, not to mention I loved this place. I'd always wanted to bring you here, but somehow never got around to it. This time, I really wanted to make it happen. Of course, the cake and all was Mahesh's idea.'

'Thanks again,' David said, looking at Mahesh.

'Hey, no problem,' Mahesh dismissed it with a wave of his hand.

Ravi gave a conspiratorial grin. 'Actually,' he began, 'Mahesh wanted to arrange for a special birthday gift . . . a very special gift.'

'The offer's still open, you know,' Mahesh said, giving Ravi a wink. They both turned expectantly to an uncomprehending David.

'I'm sorry . . .' David said, looking from one to the other. 'I didn't get that. What special gift?'

Mahesh sighed and looked around him. He seemed to have spotted what he was looking for, for he tapped David on the arm and then jerked his head in the direction of the wired fence that marked one of the edges of the resort's property.

David followed his gaze to see a stunningly attractive woman in a fashionable dress come in through a small side gate. He let out a low whistle as the woman began walking over the sand with some difficulty, given her high heels. 'Wow. Actually, I saw another girl too, in the parking lot. I thought she was waiting for her date or maybe was a model here for a shoot, or something . . .'

'Shoot, my arse,' Mahesh grunted. 'They are on dates, all right. Just wait and see.'

The woman made her way to one of the hotel cottages nestled in a clump of palm trees and rang the doorbell. A portly man in his early sixties or so opened the cottage door and, with a furtive look around, let the woman in.

David whistled again, this time not in appreciation. He looked at the two men with him and, as one, all of them started laughing. A drunk Ravi fell over sideways on to David, sending both of them sprawling in the sand.

Still laughing, David picked himself up into a sitting position. '*Saale ki toh* lottery *lag gayi*,' he gasped, still chuckling. 'Uncle has totally struck gold.'

Ravi however, settled his face into a scowl. 'Uncle. *Ghanta* uncle. These duplicitous, two-faced fuckers. This same uncle blessed us with such a disapproving look earlier this evening, when he walked past us to get to his cottage. And now look at him . . .'

Mahesh patted Ravi on his shoulder. 'Chill, *yaar*. Don't be jealous. Like I said, I can still arrange things . . . for both of you.'

David waved off the offer, while Ravi paid no heed to it at all. Instead, he sat up and chugged down a mouthful of whiskey before declaring, 'Men like "uncle" are scum. They sit in their polymer-paint middle-class apartments and give lectures on "today's youth" and their lack of morals. But given the chance, see what these uncles get up to. And tomorrow morning, this man will go back to his sanctimonious existence and pass judgement on all those he sees, as though he were some saint. And you know what? He'll get off on it. They all get off on it. I know their kind, David. I've seen many like them: the great protectors of culture and morality. But ask one of them to stand up for something, come forward to do something? Chance-*y illai*. No chance.

'All those great men, *mahapurush*, who said I was a good-for-nothing wastrel, did one of them even show up to help when my father died? No. I was the one who quit IIT, I was the one who gave up on my dreams and slogged day and night for my family. Where were all these fuckers then?'

'Let it be, Ravi,' David tried to calm the drunk Ravi down, realizing that his friend spoke from a place of immense rage and pain, emotions that he had long suppressed. 'Come now, don't let one random guy ruin your evening.'

'One random guy! One random guy! Hardly . . . ask Mahesh here, how many of these gentlemen avail of such services when they stay here.'

David shrugged, as though he did not care in the least.

Mahesh, however, added, 'It's true. You'd be surprised how easily they can be tempted. Just a hint, and they are as eager as teenagers. Morals, David, are nothing more than lack of opportunity. You'd be surprised at the small . . . and then the big wrongs that people will happily commit, given the chance.'

Ravi took up his tirade again, 'And there's nothing we can do about it. Nothing except maybe take a nice, glossy photo of their activities, put it in a souvenir frame and gift it to them. Actually,' he added, 'I'd love to do that just to see the look on their faces, that moment when their self-righteous superiority turns into mortal, middle-class fear of what everyone will think of them, of how society would spit on them. God, yes, I can just imagine those fuckers . . . Our uncle in there . . .' he jerked his head at the cottage, 'no amount of Viagra would help him then.'

He burst out laughing. David and Mahesh joined in. The lights went off in the cottage. Their laughter faded into the soothing cadence of waves washing ashore.

Mahesh returned his attention to the contents of the nearly empty bottle. Ravi kept staring at the cottage. David's eyes remained on Ravi, on the pained expression on his face. Eventually, Ravi sighed and turned away to stare out at the ocean.

David held his hand out, indicating that Mahesh pass the bottle. Mahesh complied. David took a long draught from the bottle, emptying it completely.

Then he said, 'I have an idea.'

David made it a point to make sure that he, Ravi and Mahesh did not, all three, meet again since that day: a caution that had been required to make sure their scheme went as planned. Nor had he come within kilometres—to be specific—within mobile-tower radius of Palm Grove resort. But when Mahesh called him, telling him that Ravi was on the verge of causing a public scene, he saw no choice but to make his way there.

David knew why Ravi was upset. To be fair, it had shaken him too. Not once during all these months had they thought that one of their victims might go so far as to die by suicide because of their actions. *Damn that Mehra!*

He parked his jeep and used his burner phone to call Mahesh, who told him to circle around the resort and use the side gate to come directly to cottage number 38. David did as he was told, and found a sulky Ravi and a flustered Mahesh waiting inside.

'It's over,' Ravi said, the moment he saw David. 'We can't go on. What we've done is bad enough—'

'Are you crazy or what?' Mahesh fiercely resumed what David supposed had been an argument well in progress before his arrival. 'Just because some old man didn't have the balls to—'

'That old man is dead! He is dead! He killed himself because of us, because of what we did!'

'Shut up, both of you!' David shouted. 'If someone hears us, we'll be the dead ones! Just shut up, okay? Sit down! Mahesh, sit down, right there, next to Ravi.'

David crouched down in front of them both as they sat uncomfortably on the edge of the bed. He said, 'Ravi is right, Mahesh. We have to stop. For now, we need to stop.'

'But—'

'No buts . . . I'm with him on this. We have to be absolutely sure that nothing connects us to Mehra's death, that there's no investigation into it. Let things chill for a bit.'

Ravi jumped up from his seat. 'Not for a bit, David. It's off, it's over.'

Before either David or Mahesh could react, he pushed a coffee table to a corner and jumped on to it. Moving aside a ventilation vent that had been set high up in the wall, he removed the camera that had been fixed behind it. With a sense of finality, he yanked the wires connecting the camera to a nearby power source out.

'What are you doing? Give me that!' Mahesh rushed to intercept Ravi.

'Get off me!'

'Stop that, Ravi!'

'Don't you touch me! We are finished. I won't go on. I won't let you guys go on either!'

'*Saale chutiye*! You think I took such a huge risk to do *samaaj seva* or what? This is our ticket to the big life, to earning crores.'

'Get out of my way, Mahesh or I swear I will—'

'You will do what? Do what? Do it! Do it, I dare you, *madarchod*!'

'STOP IT! Both of you, stop it!' David's voice thundered through the room. He placed himself between the two fighting men, facing Mahesh, but with a restraining hand on Ravi's chest. He took a deep breath, letting his action and the silence that followed it defuse the tension a little. He then said, 'Whatever it is we decide to do, this is not the time for it. We each have our concerns. We are in this together. We need to stick together if we want to avoid being caught; I've made that clear since day one. So whatever it is, we will work it out and make sure everyone is comfortable . . .'

Mahesh interjected, 'But, David—'

'Do you trust me, Mahesh?' David asked.

Mahesh looked from him to Ravi, who stood clutching the video camera to his chest as though his life depended on it. Reluctantly, he said, 'Yes, but—'

'Sssh! And you, Ravi?' David turned to face his best friend. 'Do you trust me?'

'Yes,' the reply came without hesitation.

'All right,' David commanded. 'Ravi, you wanted to stop. We've stopped. The camera is out, it's in your hands. I trust you to keep it safe. Go.'

Mahesh frowned in consternation but waited till a relieved Ravi had left the room before turning on David. 'What the fuck—'

'You keep pushing him, he will totally lose it. There's no saying what he will do then, Mahesh. He's upset about Mehra's death. To be frank, so am I. Give him time. Give *me* time, I'll bring him around.'

A disgruntled Mahesh asked, 'How much time?'

David said, 'A few months, maybe? Let him forget. Let him get over the guilt and fear. All he needs is time.'

Mahesh grudgingly agreed.

David left the room to find Ravi waiting by his jeep. They drove to Ravi's flat together, but in strained silence. Shakuntala had welcomed them warmly, but then had instantly seen that things were not as usual. She had let the two men—both of whom she loved as sons— sulk through their dinner before leaving them alone to settle their spat, supposing it to be one of the many they often had.

David cleared his throat and began, 'Ravi, I . . .'

But Ravi ignored him, instead popping his head into Shakuntala's room to say that he had to go out on work, before leaving the apartment. A confused David waited till late, eventually falling asleep on the sofa, oblivious as Shakuntala emerged from her room to cover him with a blanket and run her hands through his hair in a maternal caress before heading back to her bed. He did not know when Ravi returned.

In the morning, it was Ravi who woke David up and handed him his favourite filter coffee.

David began, 'Ravi . . .'

Ravi held up a silencing hand. 'Whatever's done is done, David. All of it. It was a mistake. A terrible mistake. But it doesn't have to come between us or screw up the rest of our lives. I, for one, can't bring that upon Amma and Charu. Now, are you with me?'

David said, with all his heart, 'Always, Ravi.'

Ravi let out the breath he had been holding. 'Then forget what happened. All of it. Let's never speak of it again.'

'All right,' David said. He really did mean it. Nothing, he told himself, absolutely nothing was worth more than Ravi's friendship.

Mahesh, however, was not to be so easily placated. Barely days after they had met at Palm Grove, he tried to approach Ravi in front of his office building. It was a coincidence that David, too, had been on his way to see Ravi and intercepted Mahesh, dragging him to a tea stall across the road to continue their conversation.

'Remember one thing,' Mahesh told David. 'That room at Palm Grove is the reason why we could even do something like this. And you have that room because of me. I agreed to a three-way split because I thought this was long-term. If you guys are going to be such spineless cowards, you need to make it up to me. You know what I mean?'

David refrained from commenting about blackmailers blackmailing each other, given the crowd around them. He said, not quite realizing that he was reassuring himself as much as he was Mahesh, 'Give Ravi time. He will come around. Just give him time.'

However, it turned out that time was something David himself did not have. He also had no choice but to disclose the situation in its entirety to Ravi during a drunken evening at a highway dhaba.

'A forty-lakh gambling debt? What the fuck were you thinking, David?'

David withstood the brunt of Ravi's predictable ire, firm in the hope that his friend would, all said and done, not let him down. 'I don't know, boss. I wasn't thinking, that's for sure. But here we are. My payments bounced one too many times for their threats to remain verbal. Next time, they will break a few bones, maybe do worse.'

Ravi did not yield. 'They should!' he said. 'Chutiya saala! What you have in debt, I have in savings. Grow up, David. Deal with your problems yourself.'

David was torn between pointing out that Ravi's 'savings' as he had called them, were the result of *his* idea, and continuing to plead his case. In the end, David confessed, 'I'm scared, Ravi.'

Ravi did not react. David knew the other man had helped out with his gambling debts—albeit smaller and less dangerous ones—one too many times to take his plea seriously any more.

He pressed the point. 'That last video . . . Vaidyanathan, I think his name was. If we . . . just one last time, Ravi. Just one last time, with the video we already have. No more Palm Grove, no more hidden cameras, just this one video we haven't used . . .'

To his surprise, Ravi became more adamant in his stance.

'All this while,' Ravi said, 'I thought it was just someone else we had hurt with what we had done. And, believe me, that was a terrible burden to bear. Now I see that our mistakes have come to bite us back. Damn it, David! Forty lakh! I couldn't have imagined. Perhaps I'm to blame a bit for that too. I shouldn't have helped out when you came to me for money, before. But I thought you were just having fun, that you would get over it. Yes, I should've stopped you.'

The sanctimonious tone was far too much for David to bear. 'Your fault? Fuck you, Ravi! Before you blame me, take a look at yourself. Or should I paint you a picture of how you got off on watching Singh, Dutta and Sukumaran and so many others squirm in shame and fear. I fucked up my life, yes. But, unlike you, I didn't get my kicks from watching others suffer. So, stop pretending to care.'

Ravi took a deep breath, then slapped David.

David stared at him, shocked, then lashed out with a punch to the stomach that made Ravi double over.

'Shit! I'm sorry! I'm sorry, Ravi . . .' David made to help Ravi, who waved him back and straightened up, chest still heaving from the shock, if not the pain of the blow. The exchange, however, seemed to have settled some scores.

'I'm sorry too,' Ravi told David. 'Look, we both made mistakes. Now we have to deal with them. But making the same mistake again is not the solution. Find another way to pay your debts off. I am not going to help you.'

David mutely nodded as a mix of emotions jostled for space with the persisting shock: anger, disbelief and a deep sense of betrayal. Then, gathering himself and forcing his mind to think the better of Ravi and the situation, he smiled at his friend. He let the matter go, realizing that this really was his problem to deal with, one way or another. Instead, he turned to Mahesh, needing the manager's help to get Vaidyanathan's phone number and other contact details from Palm Grove's records.

Mahesh heard out the request with just a little too much glee for David's liking. '*Ab aaya na* line *pe*,' he said, before adding, 'But we don't have the video. Your *friend*, Ravi, took the video camera with him, remember.'

David said, 'We don't need the video. We'll just call Vaidyanathan and tell him we know what happened at Palm Grove. It should work. The rest of it—the drop-off and everything, we'll follow the same routine as before. I'll go to Opera cinema this time.'

Mahesh stuck out his lower lip in thought before saying, 'Since this is the last time, let's go big. Let's ask for one crore.'

'But—'

'*Abey saale* . . . you need forty lakh yourself. Why should I take anything less than what you get? I'm not here to do you any favour. We split fifty–fifty. Are you in or out?'

Resigning himself to the fact that he had no choice, David said, 'I'm in. Let's do this.'

Three days later, David used a burner phone to make a call to Vaidyanathan, mentioning Palm Grove and the events there, without sending a video. David half-expected Vaidyanathan to call their bluff and refuse to take them seriously. But Vaidyanathan reacted with the proper middle-class morality and fear that the others had shown, mutedly agreeing to the pay-off.

It was when David made his second phone call to Vaidyanathan, to tell him the drop point was Opera cinema, that things began to go wrong.

Vaidyanathan refused to go through with the drop-off as instructed, arguing that he would not take a risk leaving such a huge sum of cash unattended. 'What if you say later that you didn't get the money? I'm not taking that risk,' he argued.

By his own rules of engagement, David should have called off the whole plan right then and there. But his need was too great, and he agreed for an in-person handover.

'Diamond Towers car park. In the old Fort area,' he told Vaidyanathan.

The old car park was in one of those indispensable buildings that had defied demolition and redevelopment despite being terribly outdated. It had, David knew, no CCTV cameras. He supposed he could arrive there early and make sure that Vaidyanathan was alone before he stepped out to pick up the money, a monkey cap over his head and face for abundant caution. It seemed the best possible plan, under the circumstances

That night, David tried to call Mahesh many times, to get him to come along to the drop point, but he did not pick up.

The next morning, David was woken from a restless, troubled sleep by the ringing of his phone: not his usual phone, but the burner number that he, Ravi and David had last communicated on.

'Mahesh? Abey saale . . .' David begun before realizing it was not Mahesh who was calling.

'David, don't tell me you've used the Vaidyanathan video?' Ravi's voice came over the line.

'What? No! No, I—'

'If you have, you've fucking gone and gotten all of us killed!'

'What on earth are you talking about?' David asked.

Thankfully Ravi seemed to be in a rush of his own and did not doubt David further. He said, 'Do you know what's on the video? Vaidyanathan's? That's the guy you wanted to call, right?'

'Yes, but . . . no, how would I know? The camera is with you!'

'Right. Meet me at XTV in half an hour.'

'Ravi, what the hell—'

'Bye.'

David got out of bed and threw himself into the shower, forcing himself to get the better of his panic. He then made his way to Ravi's office.

It took David much longer to arrive at the XTV office than the assigned half hour. Ravi came downstairs to the lobby, to meet him. He held the video camera equipment from Palm Grove in his hand.

'Ravi, I—'

Before David could say more, Ravi grabbed him by his wrist and dragged him into the open-air courtyard of the building, towards an unoccupied smoker's corner. 'Tell me, David. Tell me the truth. Did you call Vaidyanathan?'

'No, Ravi!' David insisted, now fully alert and in control of his lies. 'Now, for heaven's sake, tell me what's going on.'

In response, Ravi punched the play button on the video camera. A scene flickered to life on the small folding LCD screen, small but crystal clear, as Vaidyanathan opened the door to his room to take a briefcase from Raghuveer Acharya.

'Do you know who that is?' Ravi asked, needlessly.

'Shit! And let me guess, Vaidyanathan works for some government department that has to do with pharma approvals?'

'The CDSCO. They just approved Acharya's newest drug for sale in the market.'

David took a moment to process the implications of what they had just seen without letting any of the stomach-churning fear he felt show on his face. 'What're you going to do? What are we going to do?'

Ravi shook his head. 'I don't know. Actually, there's only one thing we can do. We need to go to the police with this. We'll say we did it as an investigative scoop. It's the right thing. It's also the only way there is to save our asses. I spoke to Jitesh after I called you. Even he is shit-scared to touch this, to run it as a news story. If somehow Acharya finds out what we have done . . . we have to strike first before they come for us. David, for one last time, did you—'

'STOP IT, RAVI!' David shouted, oblivious to the fact that every passer-by was looking at them. The security slid out of his customary place at the entrance to catch a better view of what was going on.

Ravi ignored them all and persisted, 'This is not your scared middle-class uncle, David. This is Govind Acharya, one of the most powerful men in the country, if not the world. You think he'd let a let a couple of petty blackmailers hang over his head?'

David lost his temper, grabbing Ravi by the collar of his well-ironed shirt. Ravi responded in turn, yanking at David's T-shirt with one hand even as he held on to the camera with the other. He let go as he became aware of the scene they were causing, of the security guard now running towards them, but it took the actual intervention of one of his co-workers and the security guard to get David to let go of him.

Straightening his shirt, Ravi turned on his heel and disappeared into the building, heading up to XTV.

A stunned David allowed himself to be placated by the security guard, who knew him well enough to send him on his way with a gentle admonishment that squabbles between friends were common, but he ought to have known better than to get physical. He then headed home, looking around as he always did for the goons sent after him to collect on his debts. If he did not fix this, he realized, they would be the least of his worries. He called Mahesh twice on the way, then gave up on the idea. Something told him that Mahesh had either absconded or was already dead, probably the latter.

Back in the quiet and familiar setting of his apartment, David set his mind to the task of staying alive. He guessed he had until evening to figure a way out of this mess. Vaidyanathan's insistence on changing the drop-off point now made sense to David, based on what he had just learned about the man's connection to Govind Acharya. In all probability, the meeting at Diamond Towers was a death trap.

On the other hand, he reasoned, if Vaidyanathan was indeed going to pay up, David *needed* that money. Without it, he was dead anyway.

There's only one way out of this.

At around six in the evening, David called Ravi. To his surprise, Ravi picked up the call.

'Hello, David.'

'Ravi. I'm sorry. I shouldn't have—'

'Never mind, yaar. I shouldn't have spoken to you the way I did, either.'

David sighed, then said, 'You're right. We should go to the police. Hopefully they won't ask too many questions, given that we both are from the press. They'll buy the investigative journalism story.' He waited, unsure of the likely response.

'I'm glad you're with me on this, David. I'll admit, it'll carry more credence coming from two of us.'

'So, I'll meet you at the Fort Police Headquarters? Best we go straight to the higher-ups on this one . . .'

'Yes, yes. Fort sounds like a good idea; we can go straight to the commissioner.'

David said, trying to keep his tone as casual as he could, 'Why don't I meet you at Diamond Towers, the old multi-storey car park behind the commissioner's office at 8 p.m.? We can go together from there . . .'

Silence. David wondered if Ravi had seen through his ruse.

'Okay.'

'Thank you, Ravi.'

Those were the last words David had spoken to his dearest friend.

David arrived an hour early at Diamond Towers and waited in his jeep, making sure he kept low and as still as he could. He saw a few people come and go—from kids looking for a place to smoke a joint to a man in a Mercedes Benz who did not believe in paid parking— but no one who even remotely looked like Vaidyanathan. A little before 8 p.m., he saw Ravi drive past, to park at the other end of the lot. David felt his mobile phone buzz, as Ravi then tried to call him. He switched his phone off and waited.

Ravi got out of his vehicle, his eyes still on his mobile as he tried again to reach David.

That was when David saw them.

They emerged in ones and twos from behind abandoned cars and other dark corners of the parking lot. One of the men reached down the back of his T-shirt to draw a knife, while others drew sundry weapons, including a length of steel piping. Clearly, they knew as well as David did that there were no CCTV cameras in Diamond Towers.

As the men converged on the still-unaware Ravi, David's first instinct was to run to Ravi's aid and to call out a warning as he did so. He opened his mouth, but no sound came.

Slowly, David became aware that he was rooted to his seat, that his entire body was cold. A feeling rose in the pit of his stomach, a cross between wanting to swallow himself whole and into oblivion and wanting to throw up, so that he would not have to hold the boundless terror he felt inside himself.

David let himself slide quietly out of his jeep down to the ground, strangely aware that his actions came from a deliberate intention to hide as much as they were instinctive or involuntary. He clapped his hand over his own mouth as it seemed a whimper might escape. Slowly, he dropped flat on to the ground and rolled under the car parked next to his.

From where he was, he could see the men surround a petrified Ravi who, despite his pallid face and shaking voice, tried to face off with them, asking them who they were and what they wanted. One of the men replied with a blow from the hockey stick he was carrying even as another came up behind Ravi to wrap a bicycle chain around his neck, not tightly enough to choke him fully but enough to cut off his cries of pain. A third goon grabbed the bag Ravi was carrying and pulled out the camera it contained. He and another man examined the videos on the camera. Then, assured that they had the right man, they went to work.

David bit down on the inside of his cheek to keep himself from vomiting. He squeezed his eyes shut even as the men set on Ravi with whatever weapons they carried. Professionals that the men were, they were soon done with their task, and a brief silence filled the air as they stepped back to survey their handiwork. David forced open his eyes. A sob escaped his lips as he saw Ravi lying prone and motionless in a pool of his blood. Thankfully, the sound was lost against the loud ring of a mobile phone. One of the assailants answered the call, very respectfully confirming to whoever was on the other end of the phone that they had the camera and the man, both.

The goon apparently received instructions as to his next steps, for he hung up and then set about smashing the camera to bits with the pipe he was carrying. The man with the hockey stick joined in, directing his attention to Ravi's laptop and both his mobile phones, till there remained little to suggest what the broken apparatus had ever been. Nevertheless, one of their companions acted with the discipline of his profession to gather up the various broken pieces into a plastic bag, for later disposal.

That done, the men returned their attention to Ravi.

Two of the men pulled him up into a sitting position, leaning him against the front of his own car. David could barely recognize his friend for the swollen eyes, misshapen jaw and blood on his face.

The gang leader, as the man who had received the phone call appeared to be, pulled out a bottle of cheap rum from the back pocket of his jeans and forced the entire contents down Ravi's throat. Ravi briefly came to and gagged instinctively, but before he could as much as stir, one of the men landed a blow to the back of his head.

David saw the splatter of blood and brain, a fact that led the gang leader to berate his companion for shoddy and amateurish work that needed cleaning up. As the group's low but cold laughter filled the air, David curled himself up into a ball where he was hidden and began to cry.

At length, he heard multiple vehicles drive away. All other sound ebbed.

David slowly pulled himself out from his hiding place. Ravi's car was gone. Another parking spot nearby was also empty, though he did not remember the vehicle that had been standing there. He looked over at the dark patch left on the ground, the remnants of a hasty—and possibly needless—attempt to clean up Ravi's blood off the concrete floor.

David did not dare go nearby for a slew of reasons that went through his head, from leaving behind evidence to the possibility that Acharya's men might be on the lookout for any accomplices. The burst of logic yanked something in him back into place. He still had dangers of his own to contend with.

Wiping away his tears with a dirt-stained palm, he got back into his jeep with as much normality as he could muster. He drove out of the car park and back to his house. There, he picked up the bag he had kept packed, having already agreed to cover a story at the Everest base camp, in a bid to evade his creditors for a while. Booking a cab, David made his way to the airport, where he spent the night before getting on his flight as a ruddy dawn broke over the city.

As the airplane settled into cruising altitude, David let out a long, deep breath and sunk back into his seat.

What you have in debt, I have in savings. Grow up, David.

Ravi's money was there somewhere. And Ravi, that sanctimonious, hypocritical bastard, was no longer around to stop David from taking it. All David now had to do was find where Ravi had kept his stash, possibly in his house or office, and he could pay off his gambling debts. As for Dr Acharya and Vaidyanathan, they were under the impression that the man responsible for the blackmail, as well the video that was evidence of the crime, had been dealt with.

David was safe. All he had to do was find the money— money that Ravi had earned off *his* idea—and everything would be fine.

Stretching his long legs out as best he could in the cramped space, David pressed the service bell, asking the cabin staff who answered to get him a whiskey on the rocks.

PART 3

'But above and beyond there's still one name left over,
  And that is the name that you never will guess;
The name that no human research can discover—
But the cat himself knows, and will never confess.'

—T.S. Eliot, The Naming of Cats

Perhaps it had been serendipity that David had not dropped her home that night, after she had broken down in his arms. Perhaps it had been instinct, unfathomable and inexplicable, that she had not told him yet about the money, not even then.

Charu wanted to tell herself it had been the last dregs of trust, of faith and hackneyed hope that the world and the people in it were not as duplicitous as she had once believed them to be. Whatever it had been, it had flown out the curtained kitchen window as Charu had looked at the van waiting in the street.

She had then pulled up the number on her phone and hit the call button.

'Hello?' a familiar voice had picked up in two rings.

'Anand sir, Charu here. Sorry to bother you . . .'

'No problem, beta. Where are you? Are you all right?'

'I'm fine, sir. Sir, I just wanted to ask . . . you'd said Shalini had shown you the last bundle of cash Mahesh had received before Mehra's death and the blackmail had stopped. How much did you say it was?'

The question had been enough to trigger the same answer in Anand's head that Charu had arrived at. He said, 'They divided the ten lakh in three parts. There was a third person.'

It had broken Charu's heart to then voice the suspicion growing inside her.

Anand had been stunned, perhaps all the more so, for having known David since he was a child. He had said, 'I—we need to be sure. We can check the fingerprints on the newspaper we took from Shalini. If we could get something to compare prints without David knowing . . .'

Charu had thought of the copy of *The Adventures of Sherlock Holmes* that lay on her bedside table and the boarding pass inside, before saying, 'I have something.'

Their plans made, Charu had hung up and looked out again at the red van.

We can't keep living like this, Charu!

Words to act by, she had resolved. Picking up her keys, Charu had left her apartment and made her way down to the street.

She had turned out of the gate to head straight for the parked van, throwing its occupants into a flurry of activity as they debated the merits of getting out to confront her in a well-populated area and starting up the vehicle and driving away. Before they could make their choice, Charu was at the window and knocking on it.

Smiling unfeelingly at the two goons inside, she had said with all the conviction that came of having nothing more to lose; at least, no more heart left to break or hope left to squander, 'Hi. *Kya main aapse baat kar sakti hoon?*' May we talk for a few minutes, please?

Bringing her thoughts back to the present, Charu smiled again at the two men as they lurked in the background, waiting for her instructions. She then turned her attention to David, who coughed then rolled his tongue around his mouth before spitting out blood. Sighing, Charu reached into her handbag for a bottle of water, which she passed to him.

'Thanks.' David took the bottle and chugged some water down and swirled it around in his mouth before spitting it out. He took another long drink, which he swallowed and handed the bottle back to Charu.

'So,' Charu continued, 'you were the go-between?'

David shook his head. 'Yes, I was the one to go pass the money to Mahesh because no one knew that we had met each other. But go-between? Oh, look at you, Charu. Even once you knew your brother was a blackmailer, all you could do was sing his praises, point out how meticulous he was, how well-planned and immaculate the whole deal was, thanks to him. But you know what? *I* put the plan together, Charu. I told Ravi how to assemble the camera equipment. I told Mahesh how to handle things at the hotel, including installing and removing the camera once a guest had vacated the room. Not your precious brother.

'In fact,' David noted, 'he didn't even know where to begin. Wanted to call everyone we had videos of and "shake the tree", he said. I told Ravi that man's biggest weaknesses are greed and temptation, which was why our victims would dance to our tune. But that was exactly what we ourselves would have to avoid if we wanted to get away with this scheme. We had to keep our demands modest and we'd strictly limit the number of calls we made, so that at no time would there be enough information for any two victims to come together and figure out what was going on. Those would be the rules we set for ourselves and we would have to play by them at all times.'

Charu felt something rise in her, a mix of anger and disappointment. Despite herself, she let it show, making David laugh.

'You always thought your brother was the principled one, no? Trust me, he got more kicks out of this than you can imagine. He *volunteered* to be the one to pick up the money from Opera cinema, he loved watching these pious uncles, as he called them, squirm in discomfort and fear. You have no idea of the small wrongs—and then the big wrongs—that people will happily commit, given the chance.'

Charu crossed her arms across her chest. 'And you? You thought you were doing the world a favour?'

David shook his head. 'I never deluded myself that I was doing something right or admirable. But was it wrong? I don't know. I loved the brilliance of it all, I admit. I was proud of the way it went like clockwork. The whole thing was a cheap thrill, like getting back at a bully or playing a joke on a nasty trickster, but to perfection. We knew we were mean, but we didn't think of ourselves as evil. Not till . . .'

'Till Mehra died,' Charu finished.

Before David could respond, one of the goons scratched his head, ostensibly in boredom, and moved forward. '*Oye* madam—' he called out.

Charu silenced him with a cold glance. She then turned back to David and asked, 'But then, your own greed and temptation finally got the better of you and your *brilliant* plan?'

To Charu's surprise, David clenched his fists and kicked at a random stone on the road. He raised his curled fists to his forehead, as though fighting a great rage inside him, an anger that she had neither seen nor anticipated. Despite herself, Charu took an instinctive step backwards.

David noticed. He began laughing, a deep, unpleasant rumble that ended in a hacking that was undeniably self-recriminatory.

As though to affirm the point, David jabbed a finger into his own chest. 'Yes. I fucked up. But it wasn't greed, Charu. It was temptation. The temptation to be something more than a failure. Me, the mastermind of this splendid plan, the man who could, finally, *finally*, win. And win I did. Till I lost.'

'You gambled,' Charu noted. She jerked a head at the waiting men, 'That's how you owe them.'

'Yes,' David nodded. 'One year's worth of gambling debts.' He added, coldly, 'Still a better way to get my kicks than watching men like the ones who passed judgement on us beg and grovel. Which is how your brother got his highs. But you still wanted justice for him, didn't you, Charu? Who wants that for me?'

'Am I supposed to feel sorry for you, David? Because you're a fucking loser?'

'We're all losers. Some of us have a fleeting, treacherous win for a while, is all. But in the end, we're all fucked up. We're all chutiya losers, one way or another.'

David paused to spit on the ground, a mix of contempt and more blood, before continuing, 'I was hoping you'd somehow find the money. What I didn't expect was that you would find the hard drive with it. I hadn't realized that Ravi had made a copy of the videos. If only he'd told me . . .'

'Then what?' Charu challenged. 'You wouldn't have had him killed?'

'I didn't kill him, Charu. If anything, he was the one who wrote my death sentence by refusing to help me out. I begged him, I groveled at his feet. But he just looked at me the way he would look at Singh and Banerjee and Venkataraman and all the others. Like I was a mangy dog at his mercy. You wouldn't have recognized him if you'd seen him, Charu.'

'Really? The truth is, you were willing to give up your own friend—family, you called him—for money. You're a coward, David.'

'Call me what you want. But . . .' David shrugged, 'I had no choice. I trusted Ravi to help me. He didn't. What was I supposed to do, after that? I had no choice but to try and get what I could from Vaidyanathan, one last time. I realize now that Mahesh decided to do a double-cross on me and go after Banerjee on his own. He set up an earlier drop-off and was dead well before I set things up with Vaidyanathan.'

Charu said nothing.

David waited a few moments, then said, 'So, that's it, then?'

Charu still did not respond.

David shook his head and began walking away, but then stopped and turned back to look at Charu. 'For what it's worth,' he said, 'I wasn't lying when I said I care about you, Charu. I wasn't faking what I felt. Even though I knew you were lying to me about the money, even though I suspected you were playing games with me. Maybe I liked you all the more for it. I thought you'd understand what I'd done. I—I really did . . . oh well.' He threw his hands up in a defeated gesture.

Charu gave him an emotionless smile. This time she knew he was telling the truth. His tone was not one meant to convince her, nor were his words those of a last chance. He was sad, empty and bereaved at the loss of something that could have been but never would be.

As though realizing the depth of his own emotions, David's face held surprise. He looked directly at Charu. 'I love you, Charu.'

Charu said, 'I know, David. I know you really do love me. And I don't fucking care.'

Nodding in acceptance, David turned around and began to walk away once more. Hardly had he taken a few steps than he found his path barred by the two thugs.

'Seriously?' he shook his head at them, then turned to Charu, a question in his eyes.

Charu threw the bag in her hand forward. It landed on the ground with a soft thud. At once, one of the goons hustled forward to pick it up. Unzipping the bag, he did a quick survey of the contents and then nodded in acknowledgement to his colleague.

David sighed loudly, then said, 'Thank you, Charu. I mean that. Thanks for doing what Ravi wouldn't.' He made to walk on, but was stopped with a hand on his chest by the second thug. 'What the fuck . . .' He spun around to look at Charu, the move giving the thug the chance to grab David's arms and pin them behind his back.

'Charu . . . ?'

Charu did not look at him, addressing the two men instead, 'As we discussed. Forty lakh rupees is what David owes you. The rest is from me . . . make sure you do a good job.'

'No! No!' A terrified David began shouting. 'No, Charu, please! Please! I'm sorry. I'm so . . . aargh.'

Charu turned around and began walking away. Behind her, she could hear more shouts and incoherent cries. A very brief silence, disrupted by the sound of a metal pipe being pulled out from its hiding place under the seat of the van. Dull thuds, masked by rising screams, these the higher-pitched ones of acute terror and unbearable pain. The screams rose to a wordless shriek then died in a single, dull crunch.

Charu did not look back. Turning the corner, she kept walking till she reached a well-lit residential by-road, where she flagged down an autorickshaw and got in. Sitting back in the autorickshaw, Charu let out a deep breath.

In the distance, red streaks appeared against the fading grey of the night sky. On an unseen horizon, the sun began to rise.

ACKNOWLEDGEMENTS

Putting together a book during the pandemic was no easy task, and we are grateful to the many individuals whose hard work has gone into placing this book in the hands of the readers.

Milee Ashwarya and Saksham Garg for all their dedication and direction.

Saloni Mital, Radhika Agarwal and Anuj Pant for the many rounds of editing—your keen eye and commitment to detail is much appreciated!

Pallavi Narayan for proofreading, Kafeel Ahmad for typesetting it so elegantly, Akangksha Sarmah for the stunning cover, Chetan Joshi for managing the production so seamlessly, Lipika Bhushan and Chhaya Sharma for letting the world know about this book, and Lisamma Kuriakose and Rachna Pratap for making accounting and contracts so painless.

Thanks also to the other individuals at Penguin Random House India whom we may not have interacted with directly. Please know that your work is much appreciated.

Jayapriya Vasudevan of Jacaranda Agency for helping this book find a home.

We are also grateful to Vivek Rangachari for his feedback on an earlier draft of the concept.

Finally, we would also like to thank the reading community—booksellers, distributors, readers, reviewers and all the others involved. These times have not been easy on us all and we are truly appreciative of your efforts.

Stay safe!